Hippocrene Insiders' Guide to
DOMINICAN REPUBLIC

Hippocrene Insiders' Guide to
DOMINICAN REPUBLIC

Jack Tucker
Ursula Eberhard

HIPPOCRENE BOOKS
New York

For information, address:
Hippocrene Books, Inc.
171 Madison Avenue
New York, NY 10016

The views expressed in this book are the authors' and
do not necessarily reflect those of the U.S. State Department.

ISBN 0-7818-0075-7

Library of Congress Cataloging-in-Publication Data

Tucker, Jack, 1954–
    Hippocrene insiders' guide to Dominican Republic.
        p.   cm.
    Includes index.
    ISBN 0-7818-0075-7 :
    1. Dominican Republic—Description and travel—1981–
I. Eberhard, Ursula, 1954–   . II. Title.
F1936.3.T83   1993
917.29304'54—dc20   92-31226
                                                            CIP

Printed in the United States of America.

Contents

Maps

The Dominican Republic

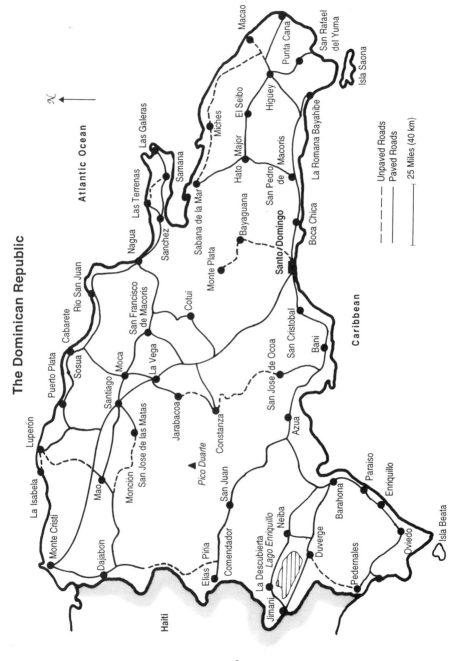

Atlantic Ocean

Haiti

Caribbean

Macao
San Rafael del Yuma
Punta Cana
Isla Saona
El Seibo
Higüey
Miches
Hato Major
La Romana Bayahibe
San Pedro de Macoris
Las Galeras
Samana
Sabana de la Mar
Boca Chica
Las Terrenas
Sanchez
Bayaguana
Santo/Domingo
Nagua
Monte Plata
Rio San Juan
Cabarete
San Francisco de Macoris
Cotui
Puerto Plata
Sosua
Moca
La Vega
San Cristobal
Bani
San Jose de Ocoa
Luperón
Santiago
Jarabacoa
Azua
San Jose de las Matas
Constanza
Pico Duarte
La Isabela
Mao
Moncion
San Juan
Paraiso
Enriquillo
Monte Cristi
Dajabon
Elias Piña
Comendador
Neiba
Barahona
Lago Enriquillo
Duverge
Oviedo
Isla Beata
Jimani
La Descubierta
Pedernales

Unpaved Roads
Paved Roads
25 Miles (40 km)

6

CHAPTER 1

Basic Information

The Dominican Republic is already a tourist mecca with beautiful beaches and a year-around tropical climate. However, most visitors have only a limited sense of what is available and miss the opportunity to see many of the most interesting parts of the country. This is no minuscule Caribbean island. Many people don't realize this country is twice as large as Massachusetts or New Jersey and is more than five times as large as Puerto Rico! This country has excellent beach resorts and this book provides all the information needed for beach vacations. However, we also believe it is important to include information for those visitors seeking to explore the country's historic sites and fantastic national parks.

Although tourist resorts have been set up near Puerto Plata on the north coast and to the east of Santo Domingo, scant attention has been paid to developing other coastal areas or the central mountain region. These are areas with great tourist potential, fascinating flora and fauna, and dramatic variations in climate. Entrepreneurs in the tourism sector have focused on the beaches and have yet to make an effort to develop the country's hiking and mountaineering potential. Basic information needed to explore these areas is unavailable locally. Most road maps of the country are unreliable to the point where travelers in the interior cannot tell if a given road is paved. Road signs are largely inaccurate and non-Spanish speakers are at a considerable disadvantage.

But, this country has one of the most impressive networks of national parks in Latin America. National parks and nature reserves cover more than 5500 square km. (2124 square miles), more than 10 percent of the country's area. These parks are home to a wide variety of plants and animals that most visitors don't even know about, let alone see. The parks are virtually hidden in remote areas with few signs or designated trails. The essential problem facing visitors to the Dominican Republic is getting good information; everything is available if you know where to go and what to do. This book provides that information in a coherent and user-friendly way.

Beaches

The country's long coastline offers a broad choice to beach enthusiasts. The coast varies from steep cliffs to strong surf pebble beaches, to quiet sandy beaches protected by reefs. Much of the coast is lined with palms and mangrove trees. The resorts with the highest quality and best service tend to be in Playa Dorada on the north coast (Chapter 4), as well as the southeast coast and Punta Cana (Chapter 9). Las Terrenas and Las Galeras on the Samana peninsula (Chapter 5) provide somewhat less expensive and more remote beach options. Sosua (Chapter 4) with lots of reasonable accommodations and an enjoyable, if somewhat crowded, beach area is well suited for budget travelers. Few foreign tourists visit Monte Cristi in the northwest (Chapter 4) or the southwest coast with their remote beaches and rustic (but cheap) hotels.

Mountains

The main two mountain towns are Jarabocoa and Constanza (Chapter 10) which are much cooler than the coast and have completely different flora (mostly pines). There are two large national parks in this area from where visitors can climb Pico Duarte and La Pelona, the highest mountains in the Caribbean (above 3,050 m. or 10,000 ft.). Other enjoyable mountain towns are San Jose de las Matas (Chapter 6) and San Jose de Ocoa (Chapter 7). Near the Haitian border in the southwest the Sierra de Baoruco National Park (Chapter 7) provides excellent mountain hiking.

Historic Sites

The colonial zone in Santo Domingo (Chapter 8) contains many 16th century churches, buildings and museums including the palace of Diego Columbus, Christopher's son. For visitors with a keen sense of history a visit to La Isabela (Chapter 4), the ruins of the first European settlement in the Americas, is well worth the effort. Another place of great historical significance is Santo Cerro (Chapter 6) where Columbus defeated the Taino in 1495, a feat still commemorated by an annual religious pilgrimage. Ancient Taino petroglyphs can still be seen in remote caves in Los Haitises and Jaragua National Parks as well as in rock outcrops along Lago Enriquillo and near Pico Duarte.

Travel to Haiti

Traveling between the Dominican Republic and Haiti is possible through either Jimani (Chapter 7) or through Dajabon (Chapter 4) in the north. Requests for bribes are not unheard of at the border and travelers are advised not to travel across with their own vehicles. Inexpensive Haitian buses regularly travel back and forth between Santo Domingo and Port-au-Prince by way of Jimani. Alternatively, organized tours often make the crossing via Dajabon to visit Cap Haitien and the Citadel. There are also regular flights from Santo Domingo to Port-au-Prince.

Dominican Culture

Although generalizing about entire peoples is somewhat hazardous and superficial, a few basic points can be usefully made for the benefit of travelers completely unfamiliar with the country. Despite repeated U.S. government involvement in Dominican politics (Chapter 3) anti-American sentiment is virtually nonexistent. Many Dominicans have family ties to the United States, especially in the New York and Miami areas, and identify with U.S. culture. Critical comments about New York City will not make you popular here. Middle class Dominicans have access to several U.S. cable television channels and watch many popular U.S. programs in English. More affluent Dominicans in business or the tourism sector often speak English, although the bulk of the population does not. It is significantly more difficult to find your way around using only English than it would be, for example, in Western Europe. However, the Dominicans are tolerant listeners and will do their best to understand less than fluent Spanish.

Political opposition is freely expressed and sharply critical comments about the Dominican government are not uncommon. The police and military are under firm civilian control and represent a serious problem only for visitors involved in the use of illicit drugs—which should be avoided at all costs. Unfortunately, it is not uncommon for the police along major roads to stop cars, allegedly for speeding, and to accept small bribes to overlook the "speeding" infraction. While this practice is an irritating inconvenience, it should not be taken very seriously and does not put visitors in any danger.

One topic likely to irritate Dominicans is criticism of their treatment of Haitian sugar cane workers. Allegations of mistreatment have received a great deal of press coverage in the United

States and are widely regarded by Dominicans as patently false. Another mistake visitors should avoid is asking Dominicans they meet whether, perhaps due to their appearance, they are of Haitian ancestry.

Dominicans are great party goers and dancers, and visitors have ample opportunity to join in at local discos (the best ones are often in the upscale hotels) or during festivals. Merengue is very much the national music and is extremely popular. Dominicans tend to play music at a much higher volume than would be the case in mainstream America, perhaps to create a more all-encompassing mood. Sexual mores are not strict for either men or women, a fact travelers should carefully take into account during their visits.

Dominicans are generally quite friendly and helpful (especially in rural areas), once contact has been made. Shopkeepers and local guides contacted through hotels can be very informative. Unfortunately the country's relative poverty creates a situation where trinket vendors and beggars gather in areas frequented by tourists, especially in Santo Domingo's colonial zone. It is important to remember these people are not typical Dominicans and often represent the worst elements.

Using This Guidebook

This guidebook is designed to enable travelers to see the Dominican Republic on their own, even if they have only a limited ability to speak Spanish. Chapter 2 covers various practical information and Chapter 3 provides an historical overview of major developments in the country. The other seven chapters divide the Dominican Republic into seven regions and include specific travel information (with maps) needed by visitors to find their ways without having to rely on road signs or guides. The comprehensive list of hotels in Appendix A corresponds with the text and includes luxury beach resorts as well as very basic accommodations for the budget traveler.

CHAPTER 2

Practical Information

Arrival

Citizens of the United States, Canada and most European countries do not need visas and can enter the country with passports. Visitors are required to purchase tourist cards which cost $10 and can be obtained at the airport on arrival. A $10 departure tax also must be paid by departing tourists. Customs and immigration procedures are usually not particularly onerous.

American Airlines is by far the largest U.S. carrier serving the country and flights arrive daily from New York, Miami and San Juan, Puerto Rico. Daily flights arrive from Europe with Iberia and various charter services. Most international flights arrive at Santo Domingo's Las Americas airport, 25 km. (16 miles) east of the city on the coast, but a significant number also stop at Puerto Plata on the north coast. Numerous charter flights filled with sun-seeking northerners arrive in this country, many bypassing Santo Domingo in favor of Puerto Plata or Punta Cana airport (see Chapter 9).

Shopping and Customs

U.S. citizens returning to the States from the Dominican Republic can bring back up to $400 of duty-free goods if they have been out of the U.S. for at least 48 hours and have not used this duty-free privilege in the last 30 days. In addition, up to $50 in gifts can be sent back from the Dominican Republic each day provided not more than one gift per day is sent to the same address. The liquor allowance is 1 liter (33.8 fluid ounces) duty-free. Five cartons of cigarettes are duty-free, any additional cigarettes are taxed at a rate of $.80 per carton. No tobacco products from Cuba can be imported into the U.S. Shoppers exceeding the $400 duty-free quota must pay a straight 10 percent tax on the first $1,000 worth of merchandise above the quota.

Most personal belongings can be brought into the country without difficulty. Sophisticated electronic equipment such as TVs, stereos, and certain cameras must be declared. Special permits are required for plants, meat products, live animals and shot guns. Trade in certain drugs, antiques, gold, semi-precious stones and archeological objects is restricted. Sea turtles are on the list of endangered animals and are subject to confiscation upon returning to the U.S. Duty-free shopping is possible at all airports and in duty-free shops in Santo Domingo.

Ceramics come to the capital from places in the interior of the country such as Banao. The most famous ceramic piece is the *Dama Criolla*—a woman in a long Spanish dress carrying a basket of fruit on her head. Wooden carvings, often made from mahogany, of birds, reptiles, ancient Taino figures and carnival masks are quite popular. Mercado Modelo (Chapter 8) is a good place to buy these items at reasonable prices.

There are numerous reputable art galleries in Santo Domingo

where a variety of colorful paintings are on display. Many of these paintings are Haitian primitives which vary widely in quality.

Dominican Semi-precious Stones: Larimar and Amber

Visitors to the Dominican Republic will be pleased to learn this island is replete with stone treasures: the deep yellow of ancient amber and the many-faceted blues of larimar. Both stones are made into jewelry and sold locally. Good places to purchase amber and larimar are Plaza Criolla (Chapter 8), the Amber Museum in Puerto Plata or Ambar Nacional in Santo Domingo's colonial zone (on the corner of Restauracion and Hostos).

Amber

Amber is an old world gem which has been popular for its beauty and ease of carving since the time of the ancient Egyptians. Amber was widely believed by early man to be captured sunlight. Traditionally the principal source of amber has been the Baltic region, but the Dominican Republic is also richly endowed with amber deposits (see Chapter 4, Amber Museum). Amber comes from prehistoric tree sap produced by the thick pine forests which covered what is now Hispaniola 25 to 40 million years ago. This tree sap was altered by heat and pressure over millions of years into stone.

Dominican amber is slightly softer than Baltic amber, measuring 1.5 to 2.0 on the Moh hardness scale. Although usually yellow or brown, Dominican amber is occasionally found in other colors (such as red and blue) which are very expensive due to their rarity. The Spaniards discovered amber on Hispaniola in 1496, during Columbus' second voyage. Since 1947 amber has been produced commercially from mines currently operating in the Santiago, Puerto Plata, Tamboril and Bayaguana areas. Amber has also provided scientists with invaluable information in preserved fossils of earlier life forms. In 1989 a piece of Dominican amber conclusively proved that mushrooms are 40 million years old, twice as old as previously believed.

Larimar

Larimar, a blue-colored variant of the mineral pectolite, is found only in the Dominican Republic. This unique stone's color ranges from deep sky blue to blue green and is the result of contact with copper and cobalt oxide during its geological formation. The earliest known reference to larimar in English was in 1974 by Norman Rillings, a Peace Corps volunteer. By 1975 larimar began appearing in Dominican jewelry stores. The name is said to have originated with one of the first commercial suppliers, Miguel Mendez. He named the gem after his daughter Lari and its sea blue color (*mar* means ocean in Spanish). Larimar is mined by hand in remote open pits near Sierra de Baoruco (Chapter 7) and sold through a miners' cooperative. Larimar is priced according to color and purity, i.e., the clearer the blue the higher the price.

Internal Transportation

Most visitors to Santo Domingo are surprised by the lack of taxis cruising along the streets. In fact public transportation is everywhere, offered by unmarked *conchos* and *publicos* which travel fixed routes and cram in as many people as possible as they go. The fares are very low by U.S. standards, but the ride is apt to be slow and uncomfortable. There is no middle-class system of roving taxis hired by individuals, and radio taxis are available only by calling cab companies. Taxi companies offering 24-hour radio service include: Taxi Raffi (685-2268/689-5468), Apolo Taxi (541-9595/531-3800), Bravo Taxi (686-1397), Micro-Movil (689-6141), Terra Taxi (541-2525) and Tropi Taxi (531-3991). Taxis are also available at airports and major tourist hotels. It is a good idea to agree on a fare in advance with the taxi driver. Many resort hotels post taxi rates at the entrance of the hotel and can assist in arranging for a taxi. Drivers and hourly fares can also be arranged. It is customary to tip the driver a few pesos.

Reasonably priced bus service is available between major Dominican towns. The best bet for most travelers is probably Metro Servicios Turisticos (Winston Churchill Avenue at the corner of Hatuey near 27 de Febrero, tel. 566-7126/566-6590) which has daily bus service to Santiago, Nagua, San Francisco de Macoris, Castillo, La Vega, Moca and Puerto Plata. Comfortable air-conditioned rides cost about US$12 and take about 4 hours from Santo Domingo to Puerto Plata. Alternatively Caribe Tours (27 de Febrero Avenue at the corner of Leopoldo Navarro street, tel. 687-3171/78) also provides scheduled service but is somewhat less organized than Metro. Making reservations in advance is advisable, especially on weekends.

Car rentals tend to start at roughly US$75 per day, relatively high by international standards. Numerous car rental agencies have offices in the larger hotels and at the major airports. Most rent mainly Japanese cars, ranging from economic compacts to sedan models. Both automatic and standard shifts, as well as air-conditioning, are available. Insurance coverage is an additional charge. No deposit is generally required for travelers with credit cards. International or U.S. drivers' licenses are usually sufficient, although some agencies require the renter to be at least 25-years-old. Some of the major car rental agencies are:

Budget:	Santo Domingo	567-0175, 562-6812
	Int. Airport Santo Domingo	549-0351
	Int. Airport Puerto Plata	586-0284
	Puerto Plata	586-4433
Dollar:	Sheraton Santo Domingo	689-5329
Hertz:	Av. Independencia (S.D.)	688-2277
	Int. Airport Santo Domingo	685-1216
	Int. Airport Puerto Plata	586-0200
Avis:	Hotel Santo Domingo	535-1511, 533-3530
	Hotel Hispaniola	535-7111

	Int. Airport Santo Domingo	549-0468
	Int. Airport Puerto Plata	586-4436
Thrifty:	Av. Bolivar 452, S.D.	687-9369
	Int. Airport Santo Domingo	549-0717
	Int. Airport Puerto Plata	586-0242

In tourist areas on the north and south coasts motor scooters can also be rented. Motor scooter rentals sometimes entail high risk for renters because insurance is often unavailable and theft is a problem. Better terms may be available at certain tourist hotels.

Alternatively, the budget traveler can travel like the average Dominican by taking the local *guaguas* (buses) which stop everywhere and take passengers in all directions. The drawback to traveling by the local guagua is that it will probably be an ancient vehicle subject to frequent mechanical problems and crowded with passengers. Being fluent in Spanish is necessary to know whether you're going in the right direction and when to get off. However, for budget travelers with plenty of time and at least a little Spanish, guagua travel is a good way to mix with the local people.

Travelers with limited time may prefer flying around the country. Flights for small groups of people can be arranged from Herrera Airport in Santo Domingo to the north coast tourist areas (Puerto Plata, Samana) and take about 45 minutes (compared to 4 hours by car) and cost about US$200 per person. Flights from Santo Domingo to Punta Cana airport in the east take 45 minutes and cost about US$235 per person. Recently Columbus Air, a German-owned charter flight company, began offering domestic flights and trips to Haiti. The company has an office in Sosua (tel. 571-3036).

While there are no scheduled boat services around the island, small boats can be hired in many locations (see below) for sightseeing trips.

National Parks

The Dominican Republic enjoys a vast system of national parks and nature reserves which account for more than 10 percent of

NATIONAL PARKS AND NATURE RESERVES

1. Parque Nacional del Este
2. Parque Nacional Armando Bermudez
3. Parque Nacional Jose del Carmen Ramirez
4. Reserva Cientifica Valle Nuevo
5. Parque Nacional Monte Cristi
6. Reserva Cientifica Isabel de Torres
7. Parque nacional Los Haitises
8. Parque Nacional Sierra de Bahoruco
9. Parque Nacional Jaraqua
10. Reserva Cientifica Lagunas Redonda y Limon
11. Parque Nacional Isla Cabritos
12. Parque Nacional Submarino La Caleta

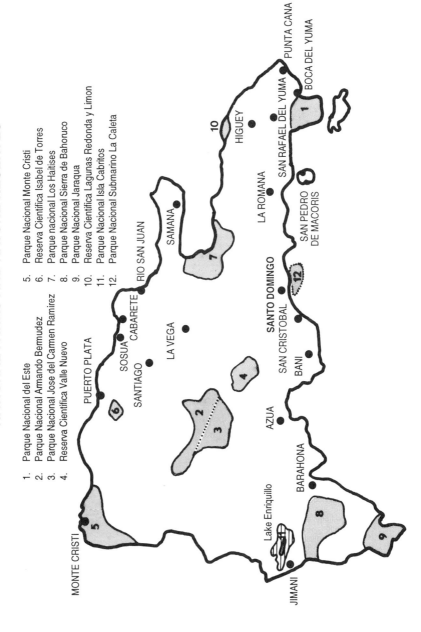

19

the country's territory. To visit these parks it is generally advisable to stop by the government's Ecoturista office (in the Eugenio Maria de Hostos park near the obelisk on the Malecon on Vicini Burgos street, just up the street from the Ministry of Tourism) to buy a pass which costs RD$50 for foreigners and RD$20 for Dominicans. Conditions in the parks are rather primitive and it helps to have already received a pass in the capital before arriving. Ecoturista arranges trips to Isla Saona (Chapter 9) in the National Park of the East that include food and transportation from Santo Domingo for RD$850 per person. It is essential for visitors who want to reach Isla de Cabritos National Park (Chapter 7) to stop by the Ecoturista office (tel. 221-4104/06, fax 689-3703).

Sailing and Yacht Clubs

There are several yacht clubs along the Dominican coast in such places as Monte Cristi (tel. 579-2530), Pepillo Salcedo on the Bay of Monsanillo (tel. 529-3383), Playa Cofresi near Puerto Plata, Sosua (tel. 535-6168), Samana (tel. 538-2587), Boca de Yuma, La Romana, San Pedro de Macoris (tel. 529-3383), Haina (tel. 532-3961), and the exclusive Club Nautico de Santo Domingo in Boca Chica (tel. 685-4940, 566-4522) on the Bahia de Andres. The Club Nautico de Santo Domingo was home base for Trujillo's famous yachts. Dominican yacht clubs are generally restricted to members. However, yachts arriving from other countries can usually rent slips and use services on a temporary basis, especially if arrangements are made in advance.

Scuba Diving

Scuba diving is a popular pastime along the reef that follows the south coast of the country at a depth of 6 to 24 meters (20 to 80 feet). Scuba equipment can be rented locally and tanks can be filled without problems. Professional scuba training is available at most large luxury beach resorts east of Santo Domingo (Chapter 9) and at La Caleta National Park (Chapter 8), where visitors can dive down to the sunken ship *Hickory*. Diving west of the Ozama River near Santo Domingo is not advisable due to pollution. Divers should follow basic safe diving practices. In the event of problems, decompression facilities are available at the Dominican navy base just east of Santo Domingo (tel. 592-3412) or at Roosevelt Roads Naval Base in Puerto Rico (tel. 809-865-2000, ext. 7133).

Health Hazards

Although a visit to the Dominican Republic is usually a safe and enjoyable experience, a few basic precautions should be taken. As in most Third World countries, it is unwise to drink tap water or water which has not been carefully prepared. Most tourist hotels and restaurants offer bottled water.

A major danger is eating fish that contain a toxin known as ciguaterra. Not all fish are susceptible, but the consequences are serious enough to warrant not eating those that are. The toxin is acquired from ingesting fish which have eaten smaller toxic fish which consume single-celled marine plants called Gambierdiscus toxicus that grow on coral reefs. This toxic plant is found most often during spring and summer months, especially after storms. Toxic fish have no specific taste or visible signs. Symptoms range from mild to fatal and usually occur within 6 hours after the fish is eaten. No specific treatment for ciguaterra exists, although vomiting may be induced to eliminate some of the toxin. Reef-feeding fish, such as red snapper, *(chillo)*, grouper or sea bass *(mero)*, barracuda, mackerel *(caballa)* and kingfish, are particularly suspect. For those visitors determined to eat fish, it is advisable to avoid eating fish weighing more than 5 pounds. However, deep sea fish such as shark *(tiburon)*, marlin, salmon *(salmon)* and tuna *(tuna)* do not feed on the reef and are generally safe. Shellfish and lobster definitely do not carry ciguaterra and can be eaten without worry.

Another unlikely but serious concern is AIDS, known as *SIDA* in Spanish. As in most Third World areas, this disease continues to be a significant health concern. The Dominican Republic's proximity to Haiti and the fact that the disease is often transmitted heterosexually is cause for concern. However, the danger of infection exists only for tourists engaging in sex without adequate precautions, using illegal intravenous drugs or undergoing a blood transfusion (especially outside the capital). Danger of infection does not come from eating local food or having casual contact with Dominicans. Those travelers who might be tempted to engage in sexual relations with the local people are strongly advised to use condoms. Reliable sources indicate that AIDS is not a major worry among local people and they generally do not bother with precautions. Sexual mores are not strict in the Dominican Republic, so forewarned is forearmed.

In rare instances cases of malaria and dengue fever have occurred, primarily along the Haitian border. Both diseases are transmitted by mosquitoes and should be treated by a physician. Another potential hazard is bilharzia (schistosomiasis), a parasitic disease, which is contracted wading or swimming in freshwater ponds containing certain snails, which have been reported in remote parts of the eastern province of El Seibo.

An inadequate electricity supply is a major problem in most of the country and lack of refrigeration is a health hazard. Travelers should exercise care in buying food, taking into account the possibility that it may not have been continuously frozen.

While swimming along the country's beautiful coral reefs, beware of stepping on sea urchins or fire coral. Also be on the lookout for *agua viva*, a jellyfish which leaves burning red spots on the skin; apply vinegar or a mild acidic solution to the affected area. Shark attacks are extremely rare, but avoid snorkeling in very deep water. Scorpion fish are about 30 centimeters (1 ft.) long and live on the ocean bottom near coral reefs. The scorpion fish does not attack but if stepped on its spines cause severe pain and swelling; the best treatment is immersion in hot water for 30 to 90 minutes. Sting rays are occasionally found in sandy bottom areas, but will try to avoid people; frequently moving your feet will probably drive them away.

In the event that a traveler does get sick, one of the best places to seek treatment in Santo Domingo is the Clinica Abreu (tel. 688-4411), located just off Ave. Independencia to the east of the Sheraton Hotel. The emergency room is well staffed 24 hours a day by competent physicians. Well trained English-speaking physicians in the area include an internist at Clinica Abreu, Dr. Jordi Brossa (tel. 682-2090), and Dr. Angel Contreras (tel. 688-0011), a cardiologist. Reliable medical care is available in Santiago at Clinica Corominas (tel. 582-1171) and in Puerto Plata at Centro Medico Bournigal (tel. 586-2342). The quality of medical care declines in rural areas. In case an injection is necessary, make sure a disposable needle and syringe is used, and avoid having a blood transfusion outside of the capital.

Pharmacies are plentiful and generally well stocked. However, Dominican regulations concerning the use of pharmaceuticals are relatively lax and many available medications would not be approved by the FDA in the United States.

Crime

Crime, mainly theft, is not unknown, but should not present a major problem for travelers taking reasonable precautions. Numerous instances of purse snatching via motorcycle have been reported even in fashionable parts of town. People offering to change money in the street sometimes try to shortchange or swindle tourists. It is advisable to change money at the bank and the black market is not worth the hassle. Motorbikes rented by tourists are reportedly stolen in some areas so visitors should

watch the cycle and find out exactly who is liable for what in
the case of theft.

Driving

Dominicans have a different mentality than we do when it comes
to traffic rules. It is very important to be extremely patient when
driving, especially in Santo Domingo. While Dominicans can
be very charming and friendly when you meet them in person,
they can be horrid on wheels. Many middle-class drivers carry
pistols to protect themselves and disputes over the right of way
are best avoided. The best response is to remember you are on
vacation, take your time and relax!

Credit Cards

Many large hotels, restaurants, car rentals, travel agencies, as
well as upscale shops, accept international credit cards (Visa,
Master Card and American Express). Department stores, supermarkets and gas stations generally will not accept credit cards.

Electricity

The electric current is 110–120 watts, 60 cycles, and American
appliances can be used here. The European video system PAL
is not available. The power supply suffers frequent *apagones*
(outages) and most resorts have their own *plantas* (generators).
When the electricity comes back on after an apagon, the current
often surges momentarily and can damage sensitive equipment.

Electronic equipment should immediately be turned off when the power goes off to avoid damage when it comes back on.

Holidays

January 1	New Year's Eve
January 6	Twelfth Night (Epiphany)
January 21	Our Lady of Altagracia
January 26	Juan Pablo Duarte's Birthday
February 27	Independence Day
May 1st	Labor Day
June 18	Corpus Christi
August 5	Founding of Santo Domingo
August 16	Restoration Day
September 24	Our Lady of Mercy
February 26–27	Carnival
Holy Week	varies
Merengue Festival	3rd week in July
Puerto Plata Festival	2nd week in October
December 25	Christmas

Language

The official language is Spanish. English is widely spoken within tourist resorts and in certain businesses.

Telephone Service

Direct dialing to the United States, Canada, Europe and most of Latin America is possible. Dial 1 + numbers for country, state or code + number. The area code for the Dominican Republic is 809. The telephone company Codetel is a subsidiary of GTE and has offices in almost every town from which local and inter-

national calls can be made. The Dominican Republic has un-
usually good telephone service for a Third World country. Many
hotels and most businesses use faxes. To call from Santo Domingo to other parts of the country, first dial a 1—no separate
area code is needed.

Tipping

Tips or *propinas* are expected for most services in hotels, restaurants, and airports. Although restaurants often include a 10 percent service charge, an additional tip of 5–10 percent may be
left at your discretion.

Currency

The currency used in the Dominican Republic is the Dominican
peso, abbreviated RD$. Although the rate of exchange has been
very unstable in the past due to inflation (see Chapter 3, Exchange Rates), the rate has remained at US$1 = RD$12.50 for
almost one year.

Clothing

Light weight sports clothing and casual dress is recommended.
Unless visitors intend to visit mountain regions, sweaters and
coats are almost never needed. Most people dress well for dinner
at fancy restaurants, nightclubs and casinos, although few require a jacket and tie. For men a *guayabera* is acceptable everywhere. In resorts, casual sportswear and swimwear is
recommended. It is not advisable to wear bathing suits when
leaving resort areas and visiting local towns.

Weights and Measures

Measurements are a confusing mixture of the metric and the
U.S. system. Gasoline and motor oil are measured in American

gallons although all road distances and speed limits are posted in kilometers. Land elevations are expressed in meters. Fabrics are measured by the yard. Rum, beer and other liquids are sold by the bottle which equals 0.75 liters. In some cases the old Spanish system is still being used for weights, i.e., 1 arroba equals 25 pounds, 1 quintal equals 4 arrobas and one ton equals 20 quintales. Solids are weighed in ounces: 1 pound equals 16 ounces.

High Season

The most popular season to visit the Dominican Republic is from May to September due to European vacations. However, the cooler climate with less rain during the winter and spring may make those months more enjoyable. During Easter week everything becomes completely filled with Dominican tourists and virtually all businesses and offices are closed.

Business Hours

Banks:	8:30am–5:30pm Mon–Fri
Government offices:	7:30am–2:30pm Mon–Fri
Commercial offices:	8:30am–12:30pm Mon–Sat2:30pm–6:30pm Mon–Fri

Many supermarkets are also open on Sundays.

Time

The Dominican Republic is one hour ahead of Eastern Standard Time except during the northern summer when U.S. Daylight Savings Time puts New York and Santo Domingo on the same time. The Dominican attitude towards time and punctuality is much more relaxed than that of the United States or Europe.

Travelers should anticipate delays and double check departure times.

Climate and Seasons

The Dominican Republic is situated just south of the Tropic of Cancer and has a tropical climate with little temperature variation from season to season. The year-around average temperature ranges from the high 20°s C (70°s F) during the day to a few degrees lower during the night. The mountainous areas have a more moderate climate and some seasonal variation. Average temperature in Jarabacoa (675 meters above sea level) is 26° C (78° F) during the day. In Constanza (1,110 meters above sea level) the temperature at night often drops below 10° C (50° F). The hottest place in the country is in the semi-arid area around Lago Enriquillo, where 40° C (104° F) is not unusual. Santo Domingo, with an average temperature of 27° C (80° F) and 80 percent humidity in the rainy season, is among the warmer places in the country.

There are two rainy seasons, late spring and fall, and the strongest precipitation occurs in the northern and eastern parts of the island. Average annual rainfall in Santo Domingo is 140 mm. (55 inches), as opposed to 99 mm. (39 inches) in Seattle or 109 mm. (43 inches) in Chicago. The rainiest month is May and the driest months are February and March. Rain falls unevenly around the country with Puerto Plata and Samana receiving abundant rain while some areas west of Santo Domingo, such as the Azua region, are deserts. Tourists need not worry, however, as the rainy season's *aguaceros* (downpours) usually last only a few hours. Mornings tend to be sunny even during the rainy season, with rain developing in the late afternoon or evening. Continuous rain day after day is unusual. More worrisome are hurricanes, a potential hazard from June through November.

Fauna

Large mammals were not known on Hispaniola due to its isolation over millions of years. Among the few mammals native to the island are bats, the bottlenose dolphin, sea cows (manatee) and two small land animals in danger of extinction, the solenodon and the hutia. The West Indian manatee can occasionally be seen off the coast of the National Park of the East (see Chapter 9). The solenodon is the oldest and most peculiar of all Caribbean mammals. It is a small (about 30 centimeters) creature which moves about at night and lives in small caves or dry tree trunks. It is an insect eater and is very similar to an anteater. Only two species have survived to date, the Solenodon paradoxus of the Dominican Republic and the Solenodon cubanus of Cuba. The hutia is a nocturnal rodent and, like the solenodon, is only 30 centimeters long and lives in caves and dry tree trunks. One mammal now extinct was a mute dog raised by the Tainos for meat.

Cows, pigs, donkeys and horses were all imported by the Spaniards. The Europeans also brought mice, rats and cats on their ships. Mongooses, originally imported from India to combat rats, have become a pest. Eighteen species of bats have been found in the country. Bird life is very rich on Hispaniola and 200 species are known, about half of which live in the aquatic environment. Two indigenous birds that are now difficult to find are the Hispaniolan parrot and the perico.

Among the most famous local reptiles are the American crocodile, the rhinoceros iguana and the ricard iguana. All three are endangered species but can often be seen in Isla Cabritos National Park. All snakes on the island are nonpoisonous. Frogs, mainly tree frogs, are abundant and can be quite noisy, living on palm and banana trees as well as on telephone posts. Lizards are seen everywhere and 21 different species are known. The lizards all have in common a thin, often colorful skin along their throats, which is blown up like a balloon when they are threatened.

A large variety of insects live on the island, ranging from large cockroaches to colorful butterflies and moths. Lots of spiders can be found and a harmless tarantula is seen occasionally. Frequently found in the drier areas, especially under rocks, is a type of scorpion which is harmless to humans. Mosquitoes, flies and ants are a nuisance and tiny, biting sand flies can spoil a sunny beach day.

The waters around the Dominican Republic are well known for a rich and colorful aquatic life. As described in Chapter 5, humpback whales visit Samana Bay each year between December and March. Different species of fish such as parrot fish, leather jacket, saw fish, Spanish and frigate mackerel, red snapper, grouper, eel, barracuda, sardines, and mullet are abundant. Along the beach and in shallow waters a variety of different sea shells, crabs and snails are found. One interesting example is the bugsnail, locally known as *cucaracha del mar* (cockroach of the sea), which clings on rocks along the surf. Dominicans use this shell to make jewelry.

Arguably the most important "animals" in the history of Hispaniola have been the anthozoans. Coral reefs are the hard skeletons secreted by certain anthozoan animals. These anthozoans produce calcium carbonate which constitutes the surface of much of the island, including the sand on the beaches. These reefs determine the contours of the shoreline and the aquatic life observed offshore. Many of the coral reefs around the Dominican Republic are alive and depend on a delicate ecological balance to survive. Vast numbers of sea plants and animals depend on coral reefs and protecting them from pollution and other hazards will continue to be a major concern. Coral is plentiful along the northwest coast and parts of the south coast.

Flora

The tropical climate of Hispaniola and the variations in elevation, rainfall and soil have produced a variety of plant habitats, ranging from dry areas to coniferous forests in the mountains. About 36 percent of the 5,600 plant species on the island of

Hispaniola are endemic. Among important species of plants cultivated by the Taino before the Europeans arrived were manioc, pineapple, papaya, tobacco and different species of pepper. From the higuero or calabash tree eating utensils and ceremonial masks were made. Mangos, bananas, cocoa, coffee and sugar cane were all introduced after the arrival of the Spaniards.

The lushest vegetation is found in the humid forests of the eastern mountain region. Local mahagony is abundant and was used in the construction of the first cathedral in 1540. Other native trees are the ceiba (silk cotton tree) known for its enormous size and long life (up to 300 years), Dominican magnolia, the bija and mamon tree. There are tree ferns and numerous bromelia, lians and orchids in the country's forests, such as Sierra de Bahoruca National Park. Higher mountain zones are dominated by the creolean pine tree, while the desert and semiarid areas are dominated by cacti and agave terrain. The most famous cactus is the meloncactus (Melocactus communis), which Columbus took back to Europe on his first trip. This round cactus stops growing after 20 to 30 years and then forms a wool-like cover from which tiny red flowers grow. The swamp areas are dominated by mangroves. Along the beaches are cocopalms, supposedly brought to the island from Africa along with slaves in the 16th and 17th centuries. Royal, cana, guano and yarey palms are native to Hispaniola and were used by the Tainos, as they are still used today, for brooms and shelter. Other noteworthy trees are the flamboyant, the coral tree (Erythrina indica), the African tulip tree (Spatodea compulata), all of which came to the island after Columbus.

CHAPTER 3

History

Timetable Summary

250 AD	Arawak (Taino) Indians settle the island.
1492	Columbus lands on Hispaniola and leaves 39 men at La Navidad.
1493	Columbus founds first European settlement at La Isabela.
1495	Columbus defeats the Indians at Santo Cerro on March 25.
1496	Bartholomew Columbus founds Santo Domingo.
1500	Bobadilla sends Columbus to Spain in chains.
1502	Nicholas de Ovando appointed governor; construction of first stone houses.
1509	Diego Columbus appointed governor.
1511	Regular imports of African slaves begin.
1519–32	Last Taino uprising under Enriquillo; indigenous population disappears.
1521–40	Construction of the cathedral of Santo Domingo.
1586	Occupation of Santo Domingo by Francis Drake.
1605	French buccaneers occupy Tortuga Island and the northwest of Hispaniola.

1697	Treaty of Ryswick; Spain cedes the western part of Hispaniola to France.
1673	Santo Domingo is destroyed by an earthquake.
1776	Treaty of Aranjuez establishes border for French and Spanish colonies (current Haitian/Dominican Republic border).
1789	French Revolution creates instability in French part of Hispaniola.
1791	Slave revolt in Haiti.
1795	Treaty of Basle; France seizes entire island.
1800	Toussaint L'Ouverture seizes Santo Domingo in the name of the French Republic.
1804	Independent Republic of Haiti proclaimed; slavery abolished.
1805	France successfully defends Santo Domingo from Haitian onslaught.
1809	Battle of Palo Hincado; Spain regains control over eastern part of Hispaniola from France.
1821	Santo Domingo declares independence from Spain.
1822–44	Haitian occupation.
1844	Dominican uprising against Haitian rule; independence declared on Feb. 27, 1844, by the Trinitaria.
1861	Dominican Republic reannexed to Spain by General Pedro Santana.
1865	General Gregorio Luperon defeats Spain in the battle of Puerto Plata; final independence from Spain.
1870	U.S. Senate votes not to annex the Dominican Republic.
1877	Remains of Columbus rediscovered in Santo Domingo.
1899	Dictator Ulises Heureaux assassinated in Moca.
1907	U.S. takes control of Dominican Republic's customs.
1914–24	U.S. military occupation.

1930	Coup d'Etat by Rafael Trujillo.
1935	Santo Domingo officially renamed Ciudad Trujillo.
1937	Trujillo orders massacre of Haitian immigrants.
1940	Jewish refugees from Germany arrive in Sosua.
1949	Invasion by democratic exiles unsuccessful.
1955	Ciudad Trujillo hosts World's Fair.
1959	Castro comes to power in Cuba; Batista flees to Dominican Republic
1960	Trujillo orders murder of Venezuelan President Betancourt; OAS imposes economic sanctions.
1961	Trujillo assassinated on May 31.
1962	Juan Bosch elected president in a free election.
1963	Bosch ousted by a military coup.
1965	U.S. forces intervene to prevent another "Cuba like" leftist takeover.
1966	Joaquin Balaguer wins OAS supervised election.
1978	Antonio Guzman elected president; peaceful transfer of power to opposition political party.
1979	Hurricane David hits Hispaniola.
1982	Jorge Blanco elected president.
1984	Riots in Santo Domingo against IMF austerity program.
1986	Joaquin Balaguer reelected president.
1991	Dominican government signs IMF agreement and implements market-oriented economic reforms.

The Original Inhabitants

On his arrival in 1492, Columbus found the island of Hispaniola inhabited by the Tainos, a part of the Arawak people. Columbus believed he had arrived in East Asia and called the native people "Indians" after realizing he was not in China or Japan. Estimates of the numbers of indigenous people on the island in 1492 vary considerably. Friar Bartolome de las Casas, the ardent defender of native rights in the 15th century, claimed there were 3 million. Opinions vary but most scholars estimate that upwards of 500,000 to 1 million natives inhabited the island. Archeological evidence suggests there have been people on Hispaniola for at least the last 4,500 years. Considerable evidence suggests that the Tainos migrated from the Orinoco River area in what is now Venezuela and Guyana in the 3rd century. In fact, there are striking similarities in lifestyle between present day natives in the Orinoco region and the images of the Tainos that archeologists have reconstructed from artifacts left by the indigenous people of Hispaniola.

Anthropologists believe that the Tainos on the island were divided into five regional groups when the Spaniards arrived: Marien, Magua, Jaragua, Maguana and Higuey led by different *caciques* or chiefs. The boundaries between the groups were inexact and fluid as they were set by mountains and rivers. The Spanish conquest was facilitated by the lack of political or linguistic unity among the Indians. The Tainos were not concentrated in towns and farming corn and manioc was their primary economic activity, although gathering tubers, fishing and hunting small animals were also important. Tobacco is native to Hispaniola and the Taino smoked cigars made from cornhusks. No written language existed and tribal lore was transmitted from generation to generation via song accompanied by drumbeats. Tainos played a game using a ball made from fibers and a rubber-like substance from a local tree. The stone axe was their main tool and weapon; the use of metal tools had not been discovered. Fishhooks were made of bone and their canoes were made from one tree trunk, not from bark as in parts of North America. Tainos maintained communication by canoe with other indigenous peoples on nearby islands.

Religious beliefs held by the original inhabitants gave great importance to the sun and the moon as well as various local deities, including particular mountains. The *cohoba* was the most important religious ceremony and was a means of making significant group decisions. The men of the tribe would first engage in an extended fast and then be induced to vomit by a long instrument put down their throats. Having been sufficiently purified, they inhaled an hallucinogenic powder made from a tropical mimosa plant which is reportedly still used for this purpose by remote South American tribes. In this state, surrounded by chanting and drumming, they received advice from the gods about whether to plant crops, organize a trip, go to war or settle tribal disputes. Caves were often places of worship and many Taino petroglyphs were carved in stalactites around the country. These Taino idols can still be seen in their original setting in limestone caves in Los Haitises National Park (see Chapter 9). The shaman or *behique* who organized these sessions was generally the second most important man in the tribe after the chief.

One form of human sacrifice was practiced by the Tainos—burying a deceased chief with his wives. In the Museo del Hombre Dominicano (see Chapter 8, Plaza de la Cultura) an excavated pair of Taino skeletons illustrates this practice. The (older) man was buried with the appropriate ceremonial garb and his wife was placed in the grave on top of him. Her skeleton mouth is wide open and it appears she was asphyxiated after being buried alive. Under this system bloodshed among rival suitors over the widow's future was avoided and other wives had a strong incentive to conscientiously take care of their aging husbands.

The 15th century Arawaks in Hispaniola were repeatedly harassed by the more warlike Caribs living on the Lesser Antilles. The Caribs were cannibals and raided Hispaniola looking for food and plunder. Cannibals believed they acquired the strength and knowledge of enemies they ate, although Caribs reportedly sometimes ate flesh of captured babies as well. Although scholars claim that Carib men spoke a language among themselves that was incomprehensible to Carib women, they did have a common language. The explanation for multiple languages may be due to the incorporation of captured Taino women into Carib tribes after their husbands were eaten. Tainos inhabited most of Hispaniola, and Carib settlements existed only along the northwest coast and the Samana peninsula. The English word *cannibal* is derived from the Taino word for the Carib Indians.

Discovery and Conquest

Christopher Columbus was born in 1451 in the Italian city-state of Genoa. Although born into a family of weavers he was fascinated by the sea and traveled extensively in western Europe before working as a cartographer in Lisbon. Later he worked for a Genovese shipping company importing sugar cane from the Canary Islands. Like many educated people of his time, he was convinced the world was round. However, his calculations about the distance west of the Far East were considerably more optimistic than many others. After marrying a woman from a prominent Portuguese family in 1479, he attempted to obtain support from King John of Portugal for an expedition across the Atlantic. Considerable commercial profit could be made if a short-cut to East Asia could be discovered. After the Portuguese refused to finance such an expedition Columbus approached the Spanish monarchs, Ferdinand and Isabela, in 1484. The Spaniards were preoccupied with driving the Moors out of the Iberian peninsula and unifying the country. Columbus assiduously developed a network of contacts in the Spanish government and eventually was told that once victory against the Moors was achieved, his expedition would be supported. With the defeat of the Moors at Granada in January 1492, this condition was fulfilled. On August 3, 1492, Columbus sailed from Seville to discover a faster way to East Asia. He was an admiral with 88 sailors and three ships, the *Pinta*, *Nina* and *Santa Maria*.

After more than two months at sea in harrowing and unknown waters, Columbus' men were ready to mutiny. They gave him three days to sight land or return to Spain. On October 12, 1492, the Europeans discovered what is now Watlin's Island in the Bahamas. They then headed west landing on the north coast of what is now Cuba. Columbus and his men were interested in gold and were told by local Indians to head to another island to the southeast. The island now called Hispaniola was called Quisqueya (meaning "mother of the islands") or Aiti (meaning "rugged mountain") by the indigenous people. Columbus claimed the land for Spain (as he did everywhere) and renamed the island Isla Espanola (Spanish Island), which gradually evolved to Hispaniola over the years. The first landing on the island was made on the northern coast of what is now Haiti on December 25, 1492. One of the three ships, the *Santa Maria*, ran aground and Columbus ordered a settlement be constructed from the remnants of the ship. The Tainos appear to have initially welcomed Columbus and his men, giving them gifts of cotton textiles, gold, feathered plumage and amber. Columbus was told more of these goods, including gold, were available in the interior. He called his settlement La Navidad (Christmas) and tried to make a virtue of the necessity of leaving the crew of the Santa Maria behind when he sailed back to Spain on January 4, 1493. Arriving in Spain on March 15, 1493, with these treasures and a number of Indians to be baptized, Columbus received a hero's welcome.

Unfortunately the 39 "settlers" left at La Navidad were not well prepared for life in the new world and relations with the Indians did not remain cordial. The Spaniards appear to have commandeered food and women from the local Tainos, thereby generating local resentment. Finally the *cacique* (chief) of the Maguana, Caonabo, decided enough was enough and massacred the Spaniards. When Columbus returned to La Navidad in December 1493 with 17 boats and 1,500 men (after discovering Guadeloupe, Puerto Rico and the Virgin Islands) all he found were corpses. Horrified, Columbus moved more than 100 miles east along the coast and set up a new colony which he named La Isabela in honor of the Spanish queen. The remains of his historic settlement can be visited today (see Chapter 4).

The settlement at La Isabela began the first sustained and indepth contact between Indians and Europeans. After the Spaniards learned that there were gold deposits further up the Yaqui River in the interior, they attempted to compel the Indians to get it for them. Considerable amounts of gold were found in the Cibao mountains, the Constanza area and La Vega. In 1494 Columbus launched a 10-month military campaign against the Indians marked by cruelty and slaughter. On March 25, 1495, there was a major Spanish victory over the Indians at Santo Cerro (Holy Hill) where Columbus erected a Christian cross and his men routed the Indians. The spot where Columbus placed the cross can be seen today near La Vega (see Chapter 6). The Spanish victory led to an agreement by the Indians to pay taxes in the form of gold and cotton textiles. In 1496 Columbus returned to Spain leaving his brother Bartholomew in charge of Isabela.

Internal dissension plagued the settlement at La Isabela and rivals arose to challenge Bartholomew's leadership. A great deal of resentment on the part of the Spaniards was caused by the rule of the "foreign" Columbus family. Under the terms granted by the Spanish throne, Columbus was entitled to 10 percent of all wealth generated in the new world. Political disputes and the discovery of gold further south caused the settlement to unravel. Later in 1496 Bartholomew founded Santo Domingo along the Ozama River on the south coast, not far from a recent gold discovery on the shore of the Haina River to the west. By this time ship travel to and from Spain was fairly regular and Columbus heard about these problems. Columbus left Spain in May 1498, discovering Trinidad and the coast of South America as he returned to Hispaniola to take charge. Numerous reports of conflict and unduly harsh administration by the Columbus family reached the Spanish court, and in May 1499 Francisco Bobadilla was appointed governor. After arriving at the colony in August 1500, Bobadilla reviewed serious charges of malfeasance by Columbus' critics and sent Christopher Columbus back to Spain in chains to stand trial, along with his brother Bartholomew and his son Diego. Bobadilla bolstered his own popularity by confiscating land claimed by the Columbus family and redistributing it among the other colonists.

After much politicking Columbus managed to regain the favor of the Spanish royal family. In 1502 Nicholas de Ovando was named governor of Hispaniola with instructions to restore the privileges of the Columbus family. Ovando expanded the capital's name to Santo Domingo de Guzman, in honor of the founder of the Dominican religious order of the Catholic Church. Francisco Bobadilla was lost at sea while returning to Spain when his boat sank.

Columbus set out that same year on another attempt to reach East Asia. He skirted Hispaniola briefly and then reached what is now Honduras and headed south along the Central American coastline. While returning to Cuba for supplies, his boat ran aground in Jamaica where he was marooned for a year before being rescued by Nicholas de Ovando in 1504. His mission aborted, Columbus returned to Spain by way of Hispaniola and died on May 20, 1506. In his will Columbus reportedly asked to be buried on Hispaniola, although his remains were initially placed in the Carthusian Monastery of Santa Maria of the Caves in Seville, Spain.

Nicholas de Ovando had previously administered a large territory in Spain and governed Hispaniola effectively. He was a centralizer who dealt ruthlessly with the Indians. In one particularly bloody slaughter at Jarabacoa in the southwest, Nicholas de Ovando executed the Taino queen Anacaona, said to be the most beautiful woman on the island. He imposed an *encomienda* system (analogous to Spanish feudalism) under which Indians within a designated area were assigned to a particular Spanish overlord. Indians were required to work for this overlord for two five-month periods each year, and were allowed to work on their own fields only every sixth month. Their forced labor could be gold mining, sugar milling, building construction, agricultural work or domestic service. Although the Spaniards were supposed to provide food, lodging, clothing, wages and religious instruction, the Indian population on the island declined rapidly. Most scholars agree there were between 500,000 and 1 million Indians in 1492. As a result of diseases from Europe against which they had no immunity, forced labor in the encomiendas, slaughter by the Spaniards, and the collapse of their cultural identity, the Indian population was only 60,000 at the time of a census in 1508. The white population on the island was about 4,000 at that time. Most scholars agree the Indians of Hispaniola were virtually exterminated by 1525.

Aspects of Taino culture and language remain in the present-day Dominican society despite the complete disappearance of the people. More than 700 words from the Taino language are used in the Dominican Republic today for various fruits, fish, plants and animals. The names of many towns and almost all rivers are Taino. Anthropologists have traced certain slash and burn farming practices and fishing techniques currently used by Dominican peasants back to Taino practices. Several Taino words have been incorporated into the English language, such as: hammock, hurricane, barbecue, canoe, cassava, guava, iguana, maize, savannah, tobacco and cannibal.

In 1509 Nicholas de Ovando was replaced when Columbus' son Diego became the governor of New Spain. Despite the fact that he had built Santo Domingo (the buildings you see today in the colonial zone are from his tenure, see Chapter 8) into a prosperous colony, he was removed. Queen Isabela was reportedly unhappy when she heard about the execution of Anacaona, the Indian queen. Diego Columbus and his wife, Maria de Toledo, set up court in the Alcazar in Santo Domingo with much pomp (see Chapter 8). The principal street in the colonial zone, Calle Las Damas, dates from this period. Diego was a despotic ruler who remained in place until he was recalled in the 1520s amid charges he was usurping royal prerogatives. Ultimately he was acquitted of all charges but did not return to Santo Domingo before he died in 1526.

In 1544 Diego's widow, Maria de Toledo, brought the remains of Christopher and Diego Columbus from Spain to Santo Domingo and buried them in accordance with Christopher's wishes in the Santo Domingo cathedral. In December 1795 when Spain ceded what is now the Dominican Republic to France, a Spanish naval officer reportedly took Columbus' remains to Cuba so they would remain on Spanish soil. However, in 1877 the Dominican authorities discovered the actual remains of Columbus in the cathedral. Apparently the naval officer mistakenly took the remains of Diego, not Christopher, to Cuba. Celebrations in October 1992 again called for moving Columbus from the cathedral to an impressive mausoleum in the Faro a Colon where it is hoped he will remain permanently.

African Slaves and Sugar

With the annihilation of the indigenous people, the Spaniards filled the need for labor with African slaves. Although the first slave ship from Africa arrived in 1505, a regular slave trade developed by 1511. The slave population on the island grew rapidly, reaching 30,000, more than 65 percent of the population, by 1545. Sugar cane had originally been brought by Columbus and the first sugar exports are recorded in 1521. The slave trade was a triangular trade wherein European merchants (not Spaniards, but often Portuguese) would take sugar and tobacco from the Caribbean to Europe, take basic consumer goods and alcohol to West Africa and take African slaves back to the Caribbean. In West Africa slaves were either obtained directly from tribes which had been victorious in war or, more often, from European intermediaries who maintained slave trading posts along the coast. Most of the slaves were 16- to 20-years-old so that they would have a long working life ahead of them and could be detribalized fairly easily. The passage across the ocean was a dreadful trip of about 6 weeks with a normal mortality rate of 15 to 20 percent. The Africans came from many different tribes and linguistic groups; plantation owners always separated people from the same tribe.

The work performed by slaves included digging mines and domestic service, but was generally cutting cane or working in sugar mills. One of the first slave rebellions quelled by the Spanish occurred in a sugar mill belonging to Diego Columbus in San Cristobal. Spain imported roughly 5,000 new slaves a year into the colony and by 1568 the slave population of the island was roughly 80,000. Slaves often escaped and became *cimarrones* living secretly in remote and inaccessible mountain towns. A major rebellion in 1533 was brutally suppressed. However, African slaves were reportedly better treated than Indians due at least in part to the fact that they could be resold if they remained in good condition. Dominican anthropologists surmise that the often precarious situation of the territory over the next three centuries moderated the harshness of slavery. Dominican scholars claim that masters and slaves often had to do the same work side by side so that contact was cordial and led to the birth of proportionately more racially mixed children than in other parts of the Americas.

African culture influenced the development of Dominican society and the vast majority of the population have some African ancestors. Merengue, the most popular music in the country, is essentially a combination of African rhythms and Spanish melody. The original structure of many peasant houses in the rural areas is identical to that used by the Yuroba tribe in what is now Nigeria. Dominican anthropologists trace African origins in contemporary music, dance, oral tradition, clothing and religious tendencies (especially voodoo). Many of the basic foods, such as banana and plantain, come from Africa. One commonly held misconception among foreigners is that while Haiti is poor and black, the Dominican Republic is a country where people are white or light-skinned. In fact, the majority of Dominicans would be considered black on the basis of their appearance if they were English-speaking Americans. Despite the cultural dominance of Spain, a strong African influence makes the Dominican Republic distinctly different from other Spanish-speaking countries.

Foreign Threats to Spanish Rule

Santo Dominigo was the most important Spanish colony through the middle of the 16th century. It was the seat of the Real Audiencia (Royal Court of Appeals) for all Spanish America until 1549 when other courts were established elsewhere and power shifted to the mainland. Santo Domingo was a staging area for further Spanish conquests. Francisco Pizarro organized and prepared his expedition in Santo Domingo before his conquest of the Inca Empire in Peru. Ojeda left from Santo Domingo to discover Venezuela and the Pearl Islands. Vasco Nunez Balboa passed through in 1510 and went on to discover Panama and the Pacific Ocean in 1513. Hernando De Soto departed from Santo Domingo to discover the Mississippi River. Hernan Cortes actually settled in the town of Azua, west of Santo Domingo, where he wrote and farmed before moving on to conquer Mexico. Juan Ponce de Leon lived as a farmer in Hispaniola before settling Puerto Rico in 1509 and subsequently searching for the Fountain of Youth in Florida. The lifestyle of these early conquistadors can be envisioned at the Ponce de Leon farm in a remote area south of Higuey (see Chapter 9). There was a significant decline in the Spanish population on the island as many of the most ambitious colonists sought to "get-rich-quick" in the newer Spanish colonies.

Santo Domingo was an important stop for treasure ships from the newer colonies on the way to Spain. With the apparent exhaustion of its gold deposits, Hispaniola's main exports were sugar and cattle. Sugar plantations and cattle ranches were large scale enterprises not appropriate for farmily farmers such as those who settled North America. Trade between the Spanish colonies and the rest of Europe was severely hampered by the Casa de Contratacion system whereby all colonial imports and exports were supposed to be funneled through Seville in Spain. In the 16th and 17th centuries Spain was relatively less industrialized than France, England and the Low Countries, where industrial goods were produced at lower cost. The Spanish government's trade monopoly significantly raised prices paid by Spanish colonists and caused them to engage in illegal trading with other Europeans, especially on the north coast of Hispaniola. The northern part of the island was sparsely populated and for years army deserters, escaped slaves and convicted criminals on the run gravitated to this area. Black market trading gradually evolved into piracy as Spanish control over the north coast waned.

One of the first and most important threats to Spanish supremacy in the region came in 1562 from the English under the command of captain John Hawkins and his younger cousin Francis Drake. Hawkins and Drake were privateers, not pirates, because they operated legally under letters of marque and reprisal issued by Queen Elizabeth of England. Hawkins brought slaves and other commodities much needed by the Spanish settlers and bribed local officials to permit his trading. Hawkins and the local Spanish officials often created dummy naval engagements and feigned battles to facilitate the trading. Francis Drake (who was later knighted for his service to the English crown) was known for his intense hatred of the Spaniards and took a more severe approach. In 1586 Drake captured Santo Domingo after landing near Haina about 16 km. (10 miles) to the west and marching back by land. The Spanish fled without a fight and Drake's men occupied the city for a month, camping out in the cathedral. After he systematically destroyed much of the city, the Spanish agreed to pay Drake a sizeable ransom to leave. After accepting the ransom he seized all the merchandise in the town's warehouses and even stole the bells from the cathedral. It has even been claimed that King Philip of Spain was so incensed by Drake's actions that he ordered the Spanish Armada to attack England prematurely, thereby causing its abject defeat off Scotland in 1589.

England made a serious effort to conquer Hispaniola in 1655 when Oliver Cromwell sent an invasion force of 10,000 soldiers.

The Spanish inhabitants in Hispaniola numbered probably only about 15,000 including women and children. Fortunately for the Spanish, serious disarray and conflict affected the English troops. Many soldiers had served on opposite sides during the English Civil War and were not yet reconciled to working together. The English landed in Haina and marched east toward Santo Domingo where they met serious resistance from Spanish settlers. After taking heavy casualties the English withdrew from Hispaniola and went on to capture Jamaica where there were even fewer Spanish defenders. Hispaniola would be very different today if Cromwell's little foray in 1655 had succeeded.

Spanish control over the northern coast had been tenuous since the advent of the buccaneers in the 1560s and by the last half of the 17th century the Spaniards were unable to prevent French immigration to the northwest. Tortuga island off the north coast of what is now Haiti was a major center of buccaneering. The word *buccaneer* comes from the French word *boucans* which refers to places where cattle skins were smoked and tanned. Besides raiding treasure ships, buccaneers spent much of their time at more mundane pursuits such as cattle trading and logging. French inhabitants and buccaneers even reached the Cibao and sacked Santiago in 1667. French control over the western part of the island was formalized by the Treaty of Ryswick in 1697. The principal French town was Cap Francais (now known as Cap Haitian) with a white population of about 8,000 according to a 1681 census. Despite periodic skirmishes between the French and Spanish, trade in foodstuffs linked the two groups. While the Spaniards tried to encourage immigration from Spain, especially from the impoverished Canary Islands, the French established huge sugar plantations and were primarily concerned with bringing in African slaves, not French settlers. The treaty of Arenjuez, signed in 1776, established the border between the French and Spanish parts of Hispaniola which is basically the current border between Haiti and the Dominican Republic. The total population of the Spanish side at the end of the 18th century was roughly 150,000 as compared to about 500,000 (primarily slaves) on the French side.

Haitian Rule and Independence

The repercussions of the 1789 French Revolution and subsequent slave rebellions in Haiti created great instability in Hispaniola. Spain was compelled by events in Europe to cede its remaining part of Hispaniola to France in the 1795 Treaty of Basle. In 1800 Toussaint L'Ouverture, the leader of the freed Haitian slaves, arrived with a large force and seized control of Santo Domingo in the name of the French Republic. He commandeered a Spanish battalion and returned to Haiti leaving a Haitian garrison in place. In 1802 Toussaint L'Ouverture proclaimed independence from France making Haiti the second independent nation (after the United States) in the western hemisphere. Napoleon was determined to regain control over the island and, with the assistance of the Spanish-speaking residents, reconquered Santo Domingo with a large French army under the command of his brother-in-law General Leclerc. L'Ouverture was so outraged by the help the local Spaniards gave Napoleon's troops that he slaughtered the entire Spanish battalion under his command. Although L'Ouverture was later tricked by the French and sent to waste away in a French prison his lieutenants successfully resisted French efforts to reconquer Haiti. Driven from Haiti in 1805 the French were besieged in Santo Domingo by Haitian armies led by Henri Christophe and Jean Jacques Dessalines. French General Ferrand just barely managed to hold off the Haitian onslaught long enough for a French fleet to arrive, whereupon the Haitians withdrew to Haiti. Dessalines, furious about the failure of the siege, burned down every Spanish town he passed on the way back to Haiti, including Cotui and Santiago.

Napoleon's takeover of Spain in 1808 (when his brother was made king of Spain) prompted resistance by local residents of

Spanish origin to French control in the colony. The French governor's troops were defeated by local forces and Puerto Ricans loyal to Spain in the battle of Palo Hincado on the outskirts of Santo Domingo. In July 1809 the British navy, working closely with local Spaniards resisting Napoleon, took Santo Domingo from the French after an eight-month siege of the city. The white and mulatto population in the colony at the time was estimated to be roughly 80,000. France surrendered what was left of the Spanish colony to Spain in 1809.

On November 30, 1821, the Spanish-speaking inhabitants declared independence from Spain. Calling their country Haiti Espanol, they attempted to align themselves with Simon Bolivar's Colombia Confederation. This period of "ephemeral independence" lasted only two months. On January 12, 1822, the new republic was invaded by troops from the much more populous Haitian Republic ruled by Jean Pierre Boyer. Slavery was permanently abolished and land holdings of the church and of those Dominicans known for resisting Haiti were confiscated. Emigration by farmers to Cuba and Puerto Rico reached record levels and Dominican agricultural output plummeted. Land was redistributed to former slaves who operated at the subsistence level without producing enough to sell a surplus on the market. In an attempt to secure Haitian control over the island, Boyer succeeded in bringing freed slaves from the United States to settle Samana Bay (see Chapter 5). Under Haitian rule, Santo Domingo's commerce declined and shipping dwindled to almost nothing. Spanish culture was officially suppressed and the University of Santo Domingo (the oldest in the new world) closed its doors. Civil law was suspended and typhoid swept the colony.

Unhappiness with Haitian rule grew throughout the 1830s as Boyer became more dictatorial and severe in collecting taxes. In Santo Domingo, Juan Pablo Duarte formed a patriotic secret society called Trinitaria based on several groups with no more than three people in each for security. Duarte was the son of a Spanish merchant and received his education in Europe. He was much influenced by the French and American revolutions and became a stalwart believer in liberty and democracy. His close collaborators were Francisco Del Rosario Sanchez and Ramon Matias Mella. The Trinitaria took action in 1844 when a disastrous earthquake destroyed Cap Haitien and Santiago. Boyer was unable to control widespread looting in both cities and popular discontentment rose. The leaders of Trinitaria led a small force against the Haitian garrison at what is now Independence Park (see Chapter 8), took the Haitians by surprise and overwhelmed them. They raised the red, white and blue cross-sectioned flag on February 27, 1844, the Dominican Republic's independence day.

Despite this impressive beginning, the continuing Haitian threat forced the democratic forces to cede significant power to their military commander, General Pedro Santana. Santana fought well and inflicted several significant defeats on the Haitian forces. In July of 1844 Duarte was named president of the Dominican Republic and he immediately attempted to remove General Santana as commander of the armed forces. Instead Santana seized control of the government and exiled Duarte, Sanchez and Mella. Over most of the next 20 years Santana dominated Dominican politics amid repeated, but unsuccessful, attempts by the Haitians to overrun the country. Santana and a number of other leading Dominicans became convinced that, for military and economic reasons, the country needed the protection of a larger foreign power.

On March 18, 1861, General Santana re-annexed the Dominican Republic to the Spanish Empire. From the start problems arose between the Dominicans and the new Spanish administration. The Spanish Catholic Church was much stricter than the Dominican church had been. Some newly arrived Spanish officials were openly contemptuous of the local population and their culture. Spain failed to revive the economy and restore the value of the currency. Spain also tilted toward the southern states in the American Civil War (doubtless for geo-political reasons given their tenuous position in the Caribbean) and prohibited potentially lucrative trade with the northern states. Spanish control weakened in 1862 and 1863 largely due to a Yellow Fever epidemic which affected the recently arrived Spanish troops much more than the local population. Local nationalists led by General Gregorio Luperon defeated General Santana and the Spaniards in the battle of Puerto Plata and independence was officially restored on July 11, 1865.

Dominican Republic Applies to Join the United States

The mid-19th century was an expansionary period for the United States and many important U.S. politicians were interested in acquiring additional territory. The Samana peninsula was of strategic interest both to prevent its use as a coaling station by any of the European powers and for its potential as a U.S. naval base. In 1865 Secretary of State William Seward visited the Dominican Republic to explore firsthand the possibility of annexing the country or leasing Samana. His collaborator in this scheme was Buenaventura Baez, a particularly cunning Dominican politician who managed to become president of the Dominican Republic five times. Baez was interested in enriching himself and saw an annexation treaty with the United States as a great opportunity. Various American adventurers and speculators in search of real estate profits acted as intermediaries between the Dominicans and the U.S. Congress in attempting to bring about an agreement.

In 1870 President Ulysses S. Grant sent seven gunboats to the Dominican Republic to help ensure order while a referendum on United States annexation was held. The Baez government claimed popular support but apparently resorted to so much intimidation and vote fraud that the real results were unclear. The chairman of the U.S. Senate Foreign Relations Committee, Charles Sumner, was instrumental in discrediting the Baez government and turning U.S. opinion against the annexation treaty which had been signed by the Dominicans and the Grant administration. Despite a strong message from President Grant calling the annexation a great opportunity, the final Senate vote was 28 to 28. If ten senators had voted the other way on June 30, 1870, a two-thirds majority vote by the Senate would have been obtained and the Dominican Republic would have been incorporated into the United States.

Political Instability and Debt

Gregorio Luperon, the hero of the restoration of independence from Spain, was an implacable foe of wheeler-dealer Baez and eventually managed to drive him into exile. Luperon took over as president in the late 1870s and ruled directly from his native Puerto Plata on the north of the island. At the end of his term in 1880, Luperon arranged for the Roman Catholic archbishop, Fernando Merino, to become president (and head of state). Merino governed effectively with military support from one of Luperon's close associates, Ulises Heureaux.

Heureaux, commonly known as "Lilis," began life as the humble son of a Haitian sailor and steadily worked his way up through the ranks of the Dominican army. Initially supported by Luperon, he succeeded Merino in 1882 and gradually revealed himself as a ruthless dictator. He was known as a military genius and as a fluent speaker of English, French and Spanish. Lilis freely diverted state resources to his own use, debased the local currency and borrowed money abroad at usurious rates. He held total power, relying on terror and a network of informants to maintain power. On July 25, 1899, he was assassinated in Moca by the son of one of his victims. During his administration Heureaux managed to deplete the state treasury and bestow a large foreign debt on his successors.

A period of political instability followed the death of Lilis with little progress made in stabilizing state finances or paying the external debt. The Dominican-American Convention of 1907 allowed the U.S. government to control customs collection (the primary source of government revenue) and to distribute customs revenue: 50 percent to pay the external debt, 5 percent to cover the expense of administering customs and 45 percent for the Dominican government. The agreement stated that the Dominican government would not increase its foreign debt without permission from the president of the United States.

U.S. Occupation 1914–24

Faced with the inability of the Dominican government to pay its foreign debt in 1914, the U.S. government demanded that the Dominicans accept a U.S. financial supervisor and control over the military by U.S. personnel. Unwilling to accept these conditions, the Dominican congress impeached recently elected President Jimenez in May of 1914 for agreeing to the U.S. demands. Woodrow Wilson responded by sending in the Marines on May 16, claiming to be concerned about possible German influence in the Caribbean. (Wilson's policy toward the Dominican Republic presents an interesting contrast to his strong support of national self-determination in post World War I Europe.) U.S. forces under the command of Captain William Knapp seized control of the country in short order, imposed strict censorship over the press and conducted house-to-house searches for weapons. The invasion was an attempt to secure payment of the foreign debt, and was justified by the U.S. government in terms of international law.

Despite its questionable legal basis, the occupation brought tangible benefits. Roads, telephones and port facilities were built. Foreign debts were reduced, educational facilities were developed and public health improved. The government was reorganized along more efficient lines and fiscal order was imposed. Perhaps most important, the occupation forces imparted to the Dominicans a love for baseball which is still very much alive. The U.S. forces clarified and reformed land tenure rules, and foreign sugar companies acquired large holdings in the eastern sugar-producing part of the country. Armed resistance was concentrated among dislodged peasants, called *gavilleros* in the eastern region near Hato Mayor and El Seibo. Photographs of the U.S. occupation forces and the gavilleros can be seen in the Museum of History and Geography in the Plaza de Cultura.

In 1920 Warren G. Harding was elected U.S. president and ordered the U.S. occupation forces to relax restrictions on personal liberties and freedom of the press. To promote political stability the U.S. forces sought to develop a national guard capable of unifying the country and preventing future insurrections. In 1922 Secretary of State Charles Evans Hughes and a prominent Dominican lawyer, Francisco Peynado, negotiated an agreement wherein the leading Dominican politicians agreed to accept the results of a U.S. supervised competitive election. After a clean election was held, Horacio Vasquez was inaugurated as president on July 12, 1924, and the U.S. marines departed the following month.

The Trujillo Dictatorship

From 1930 to 1961 the Dominican Republic experienced one of the most brutal dictatorships of the 20th century. Disregard for political, property and basic human rights reached an extreme under leader Rafael Trujillo which surpassed any Latin American contemporaries.

Rafael Leonidas Trujillo Molina was born in 1891 into a family of modest means in the town of San Cristobal. Trujillo's maternal grandmother was a Haitian whose parents lived in the Dominican Republic during the period of Haitian occupation. As a young man Trujillo was involved with a gang of hoodlums called the Gang of 44, who robbed stores and engaged in violent extortion of small businesses. A hard working and ambitious man, Trujillo worked his way up from being a telegraph operator to being a *guarda campestre* (a sort of overseer/guard) on a U.S.-owned sugar cane plantation. Trujillo was literate and with the help of his sugar company employer was able to enter the U.S.-controlled National Police in 1918 as a second lieutenant at a time when many educated Dominicans were reluctant to work for the occupying power. Trujillo impressed his U.S. commanders in the National Guard with his hard work, organizational ability and diligence. He received several laudatory efficiency reports from the U.S. officers and rose rapidly to become a major, the third highest rank in the force, by 1924. With the departure of the last U.S. troops in 1925, Dominican officers regained control of the National Police, the country's only military establishment.

The fragility of Dominican democracy was revealed by the 1930 insurrection in Santiago against the democratically elected Vasquez government. Trujillo, as commander of the national police, assured the U.S. Embassy and the Vasquez government he would suppress the rebels while actually enabling them to topple Vasquez government. Trujillo then proceeded to run a sham election campaign during which several of Trujillo's political opponents disappeared and Trujillo ostensibly "won" with more votes than the number of eligible voters in the country.

Trujillo was inaugurated on August 16, 1930, and on September 3, Santo Domingo was devastated by a hurricane. Wind velocity reached a peak as high as 288 km. (180 miles) per hour. The bridge over the Ozama River collapsed into the river. Clogged with debris, the river flooded and ships could not pass through. The city's water pipes burst, flooded the streets and drained the reservoir. Out of roughly 10,000 buildings in Santo Domingo only about 400 remained standing, mainly the old Spanish buildings in the colonial zone. All buildings in the area east of the Haina River and west of Boca Chica were flattened. According to an American Red Cross estimate, at least 2,000 people perished, 6,000 were injured, 60,000 were homeless and everyone was without water and electricity. The hurricane worked to Trujillo's advantage by concentrating decision-making authority in his hands and triggering massive U.S. assistance.

Trujillo steadily consolidated his control over the Dominican government by crushing any potential rivals and seizing financial resources. In 1932 Trujillo founded the Dominican Party as the only legal political party in the country. The party was completely subservient to Trujillo and Dominicans involved in public affairs were virtually compelled to join and contribute 10 percent of their salaries to its coffers. By the early 1930s Trujillo had amassed a personal fortune through government purchasing contracts and state trading monopolies. The economic depression and low private sector profits in the early 1930s enabled Trujillo to gain control of virtually every large business in the country. As an indication of his boundless egotism and growing control, the name of Santo Domingo was formally changed in 1935 to Ciudad Trujillo. At the peak of his power, Trujillo and his family controlled 60 percent of the country's economic assets and employed roughly the same proportion of the entire country's labor force. His personal wealth was estimated at $500 million to $1 billion, making him easily one of the richest men in the world at the time.

Trujillo effectively used violence and terror to eliminate potential opponents and bolster his control. Probably the single most bloody episode in his murderous career was the massacre of between 15,000 and 20,000 innocent Haitian cane cutters along the border on October 7, 1937. Throughout this century Haiti has been significantly poorer than the Dominican Republic and a steady stream of poor Haitians has crossed into the border regions. Prompted by a dispute with the Haitian government and widespread concern among Dominicans that they were being swamped by poor Haitians, Trujillo ordered the military to eliminate the Haitian immigrants. To distinguish Haitians from black Dominicans the soldiers demanded that suspected Haitians say the word *perejil* (parsley) and decapitated those using a Haitian accent. Word of the massacre was slow to reach the outside world, mainly because Trujillo suborned the Haitian govern-ment. Eventually, however, this massacre caused Trujillo serious problems with U.S. public opinion. Largely to regain interna-tional respectability the Dominican government in 1938 offered asylum to 100,000 Jewish refugees and Trujillo donated a 26,000 acre tract for an agricultural settlement at Sosua (see Chapter 4).

Trujillo's sexual energy was boundless and there were count-less women in his life. Usually twice a week a group of about thirty young women were herded into his office for his perusal. He would select three or four and they would be given specific instructions about the appropriate time and place. Trujillo did not visit prostitutes, and would choose women from all social classes who were almost always virgins. Tremendous pressure was brought to bear on the families of any women who resisted. Usually the women chosen by Trujillo were allowed to resume normal lives after one or two encounters unless they became favorites in which case they were denied any other social life and maintained for his pleasure. Trujillo would often provide financial assistance for offspring of these relationships and ar-range marriages for his former favorites with his subordinates. Trujillo was married three times, the last time to Maria Martinez in 1954. Earlier in the year Trujillo went to Rome and signed a Concordat with Pope Pius XII in which he agreed to pass a law prohibiting divorce for people married as Catholics in the Dominican Republic. In return the Pope allowed Trujillo to have a religious wedding at the nunciature with an archbishop presiding.

Opposition to Trujillo's dictatorial rule within the country was effectively eliminated but Dominicans in exile remained a threat. In June of 1949 a group called the Caribbean Legion attempted to trigger rebellion by flying in a group of armed rebels to the remote northern part of the country near Luperon. Bad weather interfered with the plans and only 15 rebels landed. Ten were immediately killed and 5 were captured and tortured to death. Ten years later in June of 1959 another commando group tried again, landing 56 men in the mountainous Constanza region. Unfortunately the rebel group was thoroughly penetrated by Dominican intelligence and the rebels were quickly rounded up and brutally murdered. The story of their heroic efforts against Trujillo can be seen at the Museum of History and Geography (see Chapter 8, Plaza de la Cultura). The case of Jesus de Galindez helped turn public opinion in the United States against Trujillo. Galindez had come to the Dominican Republic as a refugee from Spain after fighting on the side of the loyalists and had worked with the Trujillo government. He then went on to New York where he was working on a doctoral dissertation on the Trujillo regime. Trujillo learned that Galindez was writing a very critical manuscript and ordered him eliminated. According to information released subsequently, Galindez was abducted on a New York subway and thrown alive into the boiler of a Dominican ship in New York harbor.

Trujillo was extremely concerned about the progress of Castro's struggle against Batista in 1958 and spent a great deal of money trying to shore up Batista. Trujillo was livid when Batista fled Cuba and arrived in the early hours of January 1, 1959, in Santo Domingo. Trujillo treated Batista with contempt, temporarily imprisoning him and extracting $3 to $4 million as repayment for resources sent earlier to Cuba. Batista eventually was offered asylum in Portugal.

By 1960 Trujillo was beginning to lose his grip on power. Popular discontent was reaching a fever pitch and the regime was undertaking mass arrests of rebel sympathizers. On January 31, 1960, the Catholic Church ordered a pastoral letter to be read in all churches which called the suppression of individual rights "an offence against God" and expressed solidarity with the families of the political detainees. In a particularly brutal moment Trujillo ordered the deceitful murder of the three unarmed Mirabel sisters. They were prominent political opponents and the vile way in which this murder was committed, by luring them into custody in the hope of visiting their imprisoned spouses, outraged public opinion and created new martyrs. On March 6 the Church read a second pastoral letter calling for the release of all political prisoners before Easter. Democratic forces received support from foreign leaders such as Romulo Betancourt, the democratically elected president of Venezuela. On June 24, 1960, Trujillo's agents attempted to assassinate Betancourt with a car bomb on the streets of Caracas. They killed two other people and only succeeded in wounding Betancourt. Prompted by outraged public opinion in the region, the Organization of American States met and voted to break diplomatic relations with the Dominican Republic and impose economic sanctions.

Under these deteriorating circumstances a group of high level cronies decided to assassinate Trujillo. Trujillo ruled by fear and was notorious for suddenly turning against erstwhile supporters who became too prominent. Plans were devised for an eight-man "action group" to ambush Trujillo along the Malecon on his way home to San Cristobal in the evening. On May 30, 1961, plotters in three cars overtook Trujillo and gunned him down at a spot which is now a public monument to the assassination (see Chapter 7). The "political group," which was supposed to seize power after the assassination, lost its nerve and Trujillo's family was able to track down and brutally murder all but two of the plotters. In November 1961 the U.S. government sent forty naval ships to the Dominican coast to prevent the Trujillo brothers from reasserting control over the country. The Trujillo family was exiled and early in 1962 arrangements were made for free elections. Juan Bosch was elected president in December 1962 and acceded to power with U.S. support on February 27, 1963.

U.S. Intervention in 1965

Following the election of Juan Bosch in 1962 the U.S. ambassador in Santo Domingo, John Martin, fully supported the new government and did everything in his power to forestall a military coup. According to many observers, Bosch turned out to be a much less effective politician than expected. The new president alienated one interest group after another during his first months in power and was overthrown by the military in September 1963. Without serious popular resistance to the coup, Bosch promptly went into exile in Puerto Rico.

The military set up a triumvirate dominated by Donald Reid Cabral. The U.S. eventually dropped its insistence on a constitutional solution and recognized the new regime in December 1963 with the understanding that elections for a new government would be scheduled within a reasonable time frame (which turned out to be September 1965). Over the next year and a half support for the exiled Bosch grew steadily among Dominicans as the triumvirate was beset by labor and economic problems. On April 24, 1965, Bosch supporters within the military and elsewhere launched an unexpected uprising. Juan Francisco Peña Gomez, the current leader of the Dominican Revolutionary Party, broadcast a forceful radio appeal for action and thousands of Bosch supporters responded. Troops and crowds of civilians supporting Bosch occupied the presidential palace as well as much of Santo Domingo, and Bosch announced his imminent return from Puerto Rico. Fighting raged over the next four days with especially heavy combat at the Duarte Bridge over the River Ozama where lightly armed Bosch supporters prevented army tanks from entering the city.

Seeing the collapse of the triumvirate forces in the face of a popular onslaught and fearing the influence of far left Bosch supporters, U.S. President Lyndon Johnson ordered the marines to land on April 28, only four days after the rebellion began. Twenty-three thousand U.S. troops arrived in response to the chaos in Santo Domingo. U.S. forces separated the belligerents and, by most accounts, saved the triumvirate forces from destruction.

The United States intervened militarily to ensure that the Dominican Republic would not follow Castro's Cuba into Communist dictatorship. Castro had come to power in 1959 and many observers saw similarities between the Dominican Repub-

lic in 1965 and pre-revolutionary Cuba. U.S. troops were gradually replaced by Organization of American States forces from
Costa Rica, Brazil, Honduras, Guatemala and Paraguay. After
months of negotiation and intermittent fighting, both Dominican factions agreed to hold new elections on June 1, 1966, and
abide by the results. Elections were held as scheduled and Joaquin Balaguer and his Reformist Party, rather than Juan Bosch,
won.

Political Stability

Since the 1966 elections the Dominican Republic has succeeded
in operating an open and representative system without major
difficulties. Multi-party presidential elections have been held
every four years with executive authority passing from one party
to another twice in the last twenty-five years. Joaquin Balaguer
was reelected president in 1970 and in 1974. The Dominican
Revolutionary Party was able to elect its candidates in 1978 (Antonio Guzman) and 1982 (Salvador Jorge Blanco). Balaguer was
reelected in 1986 and (at the age of 84) in 1990. The role of the
military in politics has been marginalized and the prospect for
future coups is extremely remote. Armed resistance to the elected
government does not exist and the pluralistic political system is
dependably democratic.

Recent Political Developments

Since 1966, seven consecutive national elections have been held.
Five-time president and leader of the Social Christian Reformist
party (PRSC) Joaquin Balaguer won the 1990 election in an
extremely close contest. He received 35 percent of the votes cast,
which was barely one percent (24,500) more than his principal
rival, Juan Bosch of the Dominican Liberation Party (PLD). His
victory was clouded, however, by unproven allegations by the

PLD and the Dominican Revolutionary Party (PRD, led by Jose Francisco Pena Gomez) of fraud. Political tensions following the election coincided with further deterioration of the economy.

Until the 1990 election, the PRSC and the PRD dominated Dominican politics. In 1990, the PLD emerged as the PRSC's main challenger. All major parties support a mixed, pluralistic economy and strong, friendly relations with the United States. The Dominican Republic's political leadership is likely to undergo a major generational transition in the 1990s, as the leaders of the two major parties, President Balaguer and Juan Bosch, are in their 80s.

Economic Overview

The Dominican Republic is a developing country with a per capita income of less than US$1,000, compared to roughly US$5,000 in Puerto Rico and US$20,000 in the mainland United States. Unemployment and underemployment are widespread and a significant proportion of the population has immigrated (often illegally) to the New York area. Estimates of the number of Dominicans living in the United States range from 500,000 to 1 million, while the entire population of the Dominican Republic is less than 7.5 million. Emigration to the United States is reflected in popular songs, widespread visa fraud, and often reckless attempts to reach Puerto Rico by *yola* (small boat) across the shark infested Mona Strait.

The sugar industry, traditionally the single most important sector of the Dominican economy, has steadily declined over the last twenty years due to the vagaries of the U.S. sugar import program and poor administration of the government-owned State Sugar Council (CEA). Mining of gold and ferronickel have made important contributions over the last twenty years but mining output has recently been disappointing. The bright spots in the Dominican economy and the main hope of absorbing surplus labor are the free trade zones and the tourism industry. The inability of the government electricity company (CDE) to provide basic electricity service is the most serious economic problem facing the country.

Tourism

In 1990 roughly 1 million tourists visited the country and tourism receipts rose by 10 percent to US$900 million. Visitors arrive in growing numbers from Germany, the United States, Canada, Italy, Spain and the United Kingdom. The Dominican Republic currently has 27,000 hotel rooms (more than any other Caribbean country) and another 1,000 are expected to be ready for occupancy during 1992. Tourism investment has been concentrated in the north coast resorts of Puerto Plata, Sosua and Samana, as well as the colonial zone in Santo Domingo and the resorts to the east in La Romana and Punta Cana. The 500th anniversary of the discovery of the Americas in 1992 is expected to spur interest in the Dominican Republic and further enhance the tourism industry.

Free Trade Zones

The free trade zones produce goods for export primarily to the United States under the Caribbean Basin Initiative (CBI) and Generalized System of Preference (GSP) programs. The zones have been very successful in attracting assembly industries and generating employment, and the Dominican Republic has been the most successful (in terms of exports) of all the CBI countries. Free zone exports reached US$1.0 million in 1991 (more than non-free zone exports). About 400 firms operate in 27 free zones and absorb unskilled labor from the less developed regions throughout the country. These free trade zones provide jobs to people with limited industrial experience and help reduce the flow of illegal immigrants to the United States. In 1991 the free trade zones employed roughly 150,000 people and provided the Central Bank with US$250 million in hard currency. Free zone assembly companies, more than two-thirds of which are textile producers, have generally been profitable. The cost competitiveness of Dominican labor is expected to encourage American (and other) investment in non-textile assembly industries.

Labor

The Dominican Republic is a young country with a relatively large labor force of roughly 3 million people. Dominican labor is hard-working, inexpensive and capable of learning basic industrial skills. However, a shortage of skilled workers exists. Organized labor represents about 12 percent of the labor force and has been weakened by competing organizations often connected with political parties. High unemployment also diminishes the effectiveness of organized labor. Beginning in 1989 various human rights groups claimed that the Dominican government was not adequately protecting workers' rights and petitioned the U.S. government to cancel the favorable trade privileges for free trade zones (mentioned above). The alleged lack of workers' rights were impediments to labor organizing/union rights in the free trade zones and on allegations of government complicity in the mistreatment of Haitian seasonal agricultural workers involved in the sugar harvest. Loss of these trade privileges would jeopardize free zone jobs, reduce foreign investment and quite possibly spur illegal immigration to the United States. On April 25, 1991, the U.S. government announced that the Dominican government had made sufficient progress in response to these allegations to prevent suspension of GSP privileges.

Electricity

Electricity is the weak link in the Dominican economy. In 1990 electricity production declined by 25 percent from 1989 to 2,889 gigawatt hours, less than half the country's potential demand. This decline was the third annual drop in a row; electricity output in 1990 was only 70 percent of the level reached in 1987. In 1990 the Dominican electricity company estimated that only 40 percent of electricity users paid their bills. The Dominican government electricity company has failed to supply factories and homes with an adequate supply of electric power, and blackouts commonly last 10 to 12 hours. Tourist hotels, factories and even private residences currently use their own private generators, producing electricity at a much higher cost than in most countries.

Recent Economic Policies

In 1990 real GDP fell by 5.1 percent and inflation reached an unprecedented 101 percent in the Dominican Republic. During the last half of 1990 and 1991 the Dominican government managed to curtail inflation and restore exchange rate stability. Monetary policy was steadily tightened during the last half of 1990, largely through strict enforcement of commercial bank reserve requirements and reduced reliance on deficit financing of public spending. The government took important measures to improve its fiscal situation including the elimination of major consumption subsidies and a reduction in public works spending.

Monetary Policy and Inflation

In response to triple-digit inflation, the Dominican Central Bank (the equivalent of the U.S. Federal Reserve) started to reduce growth of the money supply in the last half of 1990. The Central Bank began strict enforcement of existing reserve requirements (roughly 30 percent) for commercial banks and raised additional reserve requirements for new deposits. In November 1990 three banks, accounting for 20 percent of deposits in private commercial banks, were closed due to their inability to meet these requirements. The rate of growth in the broad money supply declined from 33 percent in 1989 to 29 percent in 1990. This tight money policy dramatically reduced inflation and in 1991 the consumer price index increased by only 4.0 percent. On July 5, 1991, the Dominican government signed an IMF agreement committing itself to avoid using loose monetary policy to finance future public sector deficits.

Fiscal Policy

Government spending is basically controlled by President Balaguer with a relatively minor role left to Congress in the budget approval process. President Balaguer's governments have traditionally engaged in large scale public works spending. However in the last half of 1990, the government cut back sharply on public works spending to reduce inflationary pressure. Despite the fall in government revenue as a percent of GDP from 17 percent in 1989 to 12 percent in 1990, the public sector deficit as a percent of GDP declined from 6.2 percent in 1989 to 5.3 percent in 1990. In 1991 the government achieved a slight fiscal surplus. The Dominican government is currently reforming the tax system to reduce its heavy reliance on tariff revenue and to encourage greater compliance with the tax laws.

IMF Agreement

As of December 31, 1990, the Dominican foreign debt was roughly US$4.5 billion. On July 5 the Dominican government signed an economic stabilization agreement with the International Monetary Fund (IMF). Most of the painful anti-inflationary measures usually included in IMF agreements had already been taken by the time final agreement was reached. Since the beginning of 1991 the government has made considerable progress in catching up on its debt arrears, especially to multinational creditors such as the IMF, the World Bank and Inter-American Development Bank. After signing an IMF agreement, the Dominican government went to the Paris Club of official creditors and rescheduled a substantial portion of its external debt.

The IMF agreement is widely expected to encourage more foreign investment in the Dominican Republic, much of it from the United States.

US$/RD$ Exchange Rate

Exchange rate problems and balance of payments difficulties plagued the Dominican economy for much of 1990. Considerably higher inflation in the Dominican Republic than in the United States created an over valued peso exchange rate and a severe shortage of dollars at the Central Bank. This lack of foreign exchange exacerbated the government's inability to pay its debts to foreign creditors and hurt the country's credit standing. By March 1990 the differential between the official exchange rate and the parallel rate reached 50 percent. Over the course of the year the peso was devalued three times (in April, August and October), but each devaluation was insufficient to reach market-clearing levels. The gap between the official and free market prices discouraged certain businesses which generate foreign exchange, such as those in the tourism sector, from turning their dollars in to official channels. A lack of hard currency at the Central Bank contributed to a serious shortage of critical imports, including petroleum, during the last quarter of 1990. Commercial banks were designated as managers of the new market-based system and the shortage of hard currency abated. Bolstered by a stringent monetary policy, the exchange rate stabilized by the end of the first quarter of 1991. On July 5 the Dominican government unified the exchange rate and for most of 1991 the peso U.S. dollar exchange rate has remained close to RD$12.50 = US$1.00.

On January 24, 1991, the Dominican government enacted a new exchange rate system, managed by the commercial banks, which floated the peso for most transactions. The result was a dramatic improvement in the availability of foreign exchange and access to basic imports. Fears of a run on the peso proved unfounded due to the government's tight monetary policies and reduced inflationary expectations.

Trade and Investment

On December 13, 1991, the Dominican Republic signed a Trade and Investment Framework Agreement with the United States under the Enterprise for the Americas Initiative. This agreement marks an important step toward greater economic integration with the rest of the hemisphere. Relatively low wages and preferential access to both the U.S. and European markets are encouraging more investors to come to the Dominican Republic. The U.S. ambassador to Santo Domingo, Robert Pastorino, has earned a reputation in business circles as a stalwart promoter of U.S. trade and investment.

CHAPTER 4

North Coast

La Isabela and the Original Spanish Settlement

European colonization of the Americas began on the north coast of Hispaniola. On Columbus' first visit to the New World in 1492 he left 39 men at a settlement called La Navidad (Christmas) which is now En Bas Saline in Haiti. Columbus returned on his second voyage in 1493 and brought 1,500 people in 17 boats to settle at La Navidad. When the Europeans arrived they found that the town had been burned down and the inhabitants killed by hostile Indians.

Columbus then withdrew to the east to avoid the hostile natives and to approach the allegedly gold-rich Cibao. To this day the Cibao refers to the large, fertile plain in the north central part of the Dominican Republic. As is well known, Columbus' original reason for making the journey was to find a shorter route to East Asia and it appears he thought the Cibao was connected to Japan. Already familiar with the north coast from his previous voyage, Columbus sailed east and chose a spot along the Baja-bonico River north of the Cibao, the source of gold acquired from the indigenous people on his first voyage. He named this settlement (near the present-day town of Luperon) La Isabela after his Spanish queen.

La Isabela was the first real European community established in the Americas. The majority of the 1500 settlers were farmers and tradesmen, many from the province of Estremadura (the driest and most difficult farming region in Spain). This colony was a much more serious attempt to create a permanent Spanish presence in the New World than leaving 39 sailors at Navidad. According to recent archeological evidence the town of Isabela was divided into two distinct parts. The first part of Isabela was set up near the river where the settlers originally disembarked, and the second, some months later in a more secure location about ½ km. (.3 miles) away. The settlers remained for about six years until the settlement gradually disintegrated due to disease and political squabbling. The inhabitants of Isabela abandoned the town and moved to the south coast, returned to Spain or established remote cattle ranches in the northern coastal area.

The Ruins of Isabela and the Bay of Luperon

The site containing the ruins of La Isabela was formally opened to the public in 1992, the 500th anniversary of the discovery of America. The ruins are located in a remote part of the country not far from the town of Luperon. The town called Villa Isabela which appears on most maps south of Rio Bajabonico is not the site of the original settlement. Reaching the ruins of La Isabela is not easy and the best approach is via Luperon.

The sleepy town of Luperon (20,000 inhabitants) is not a major tourist center except for visitors going directly to Luperon Beach Resort. To reach Luperon from Santo Domingo take Autopista Duarte all the way through Santiago and continue on toward Monte Cristi. Turn right for Puerto Plata 14 km. (9 miles) past Santiago and proceed to the town of Imbert, 26 km. (16 miles). Turn left (north) on the paved road next to the Cafeteria Sara. There are signs for Luperon and Ciudad Marina. Travelers coming from Puerto Plata should take the main road out of town

heading west (marked for Santiago) for 22 km. (14 miles) to
Imbert. Travelers are advised to have a full tank of gasoline
before leaving Imbert. The road is paved for the first 24 km. (15
miles) to Luperon but then gets quite rough. Upon arrival in
Luperon continue straight (the road becomes Avenida Independencia) until passing the town square on the right. Turn left on
Avenida 27 de Febrero. (The town pier where there are generally
several yachts moored can be reached by taking the next right
on Duarte.) Continue on 27 de Febrero through town; the road
becomes a dirt track. Another 1.6 km. (1 mile) down the road
on the right is the Luperon Beach Resort. To reach the ruins of
La Isabela continue straight on the rough dirt road instead of
turning right to enter the gate at Luperon Beach Resort. (A sign
points to Playa Grande, but there is no sign for Isabela.) Proceed
along this track through the remote rural area for another 16
km. (10 miles) to reach La Isabela. The road comes to an end
at the intersection in front of Rancho del Sol and on the left is
a national park sign for La Isabela. The ruins will appear on the
right between a fence and the ocean.

The area where La Isabela existed has been made into a national park and is being carefully excavated to learn as much as
possible about the original colony. The chief archeologist, Dr.
Jose Maria Cruxent, has been working assiduously on this project
since 1987. The archeologists have successfully reconstructed
the outlines of the principal structures used at the time of Columbus, including the church, Columbus' house, guard stations,
a canal through the coral reef, and the cemetery. A complete
Spanish skeleton has been found intact after 500 years. Fortunately the area is quite dry and many particles have been preserved. Dr. Cruxent and his workers have even uncovered
Hispano-Arabian pottery of a type not heretofore identified in
the new world.

Work at this site has been particularly difficult due to damage
over the last hundred years caused by the site's prominence. For
many years the site's location has been common knowledge and
unscrupulous people have sold artifacts as soon as they have

been discovered. In the 1940s dictator Rafael Trujillo ordered the provincial governor to clean up the site because an important group of foreign historians was going to visit. Trujillo's orders were not to be taken lightly and the governor diligently had the site gone over with a tractor to even out the ground and get rid of unsightly mounds and pottery shards.

Reservations are advised for travelers wishing to stay at Luperon Beach Resort (Puerto Plata tel. 809-581-4153, 581-4379, fax 581-6262 or Santo Domingo 567-7255, 567-7256, fax 565-3084) because no other tourist facilities exist in the area. Crossing into this luxurious resort is like getting into a time machine; suddenly it seems as if you are back in an affluent suburb in the developed world with well maintained grounds, complete with sun and a vast empty beach. Thirteen three-story hotel buildings are centered around a swimming area. Luperon Beach Resort is all-inclusive, providing unlimited food, drinks and water sports for one fixed price. The hotel complex was built on several levels overlooking the ocean. The swimming area includes a children's wading pool, two whirlpools, a large swimming pool, a bar, and a center area where the hotel staff organizes games in the afternoons and life entertainment in the evenings. Luperon Resort has several tennis courts, boutiques, bicycle riding paths (with free bicycles available) and billiard tables. For a fee visitors can scuba dive, waterski, jetski, and deep sea fish. The well maintained beach is far away from any major population center and there is plenty of room to wander.

Monte Cristi

The port of Monte Cristi (20,500 inhabitants) is located in the extreme northwest corner of the Dominican Republic. The nearby Monte Cristi National Park (see below) is a major attraction and outlying islands can be reached by renting boats in town. The Autopista Duarte is the best road in the country and runs (270 km., 167 miles) all the way from Monte Cristi via Santiago to Santo Domingo on the south coast. Monte Cristi was once the most important Spanish port on the north coast, but was eclipsed long ago by Puerto Plata and is now a sleepy fishing village. Foreign tourists are few and far between, although many Dominicans take their vacations in the town. There are two reasonably priced local hotels in town: Chic (half a block from the main street through town with the only air-conditioned rooms in town and a reasonable restaurant nearby) and Las Carabelas (see below).

To reach the ocean follow the main road out of town to the bay. On the right is the largest salt making facility in the country with huge pools of slowly evaporating salt water. Despite being on the coast this is a very arid part of the country. The road veers to the right along the bay and gradually turns to gravel. Several informal beach restaurants playing merengue line the coast. The clientele is overwhelmingly Dominican, but foreigners are welcome. Ahead is El Morro, a large, steep hill abutting the coast and overlooking a good but shadeless sandy beach. A dirt road skirts El Morro and leads to the beach, and it is possible to make the strenuous climb to the summit. At the foot of El Morro is the hotel Las Carabelas, which has inexpensive cabanas and a good view.

From the town of Monte Cristi it is possible to walk along the waterfront and arrange boat trips to nearby Laguna de Saladillo or to the Siete Hermanos (Seven Brothers) Keys. These coastal areas, together with El Morro and the coastal lagoons stretching down to the mouth of the Dajabon River at the Haitian border, are part of the Monte Cristi National Park. The Siete Hermanos Keys are part of a huge coral reef known for excellent scuba diving. The park has dry, subtropical vegetation and is home to the American crocodile, brown pelican, American frigate bird, great egret, yellow-crowned night heron, glossy ibis, northern jacana, red-footed booby, willet and burrowing owl.

Dajabon

The prosperous border town of Dajabon (23,700 inhabitants) is just 35 km. (22 miles) south of Monte Cristi on a good road.

Few foreign tourists visit the town except those who pass through by bus on the way to Cape Haitien, Haiti. The Haitian border marked by the Dajabon River runs along the western edge of town with a concrete bridge over the river and a high, camouflaged arch on the Dominican side. The immigration and customs offices, located in the building on the Dominican side of the bridge, do a fairly good business as traffic trickles across the border throughout the day. Dajabon is one of two legal crossing points for vehicular traffic between the two countries.

Travelers wishing to visit Haiti are advised to be careful taking vehicles across the border. While it is legal to take across vehicles registered in one country to the other for up to thirty days, cars have been illegally imported into the Dominican Republic this way and border officials may prove difficult. On the Haitian side of the border, no paved roads exist and it is extremely difficult to find your way around. Depending on who is on duty, vigorous efforts are often made by lower level Haitian officials to extort money from travelers, especially those in private vehicles. Travelers crossing to Haiti are advised to exercise caution especially when using their own vehicles. Crossing the border as part of an organized tour group should present no problem.

The border follows the Dajabon River and travelers will probably notice local people, both Haitians and Dominicans, crossing the river without hindrance. Military personnel patrol the Dominican border, but it is not difficult for individuals to slip through. The road which appears on most maps running along the border south from Dajabon is basically a narrow dirt track south of Restauracion and is not recommended. Few people and virtually no civilians (except for smugglers) take this route. The road itself forms the border with markers on one side for Haiti and the other for the Dominican Republic—there is no fence. Travelers coming this way will attract unwanted attention from the Dominican military and absolutely no services are available before the paved road east toward San Juan de la Maguana.

Dajabon has a number of cheap and very basic hotels designed for Haitian and Dominican transients, but none designed for foreign tourists. Inexpensive local places include Juan Calvo and Rosario.

Puerto Plata

The historic town of Puerto Plata is the largest port on the north coast and a major tourist destination. Founded in 1502 as "Ciudad de San Felipe de Puerto Plata" (St. Philip City of the Silver Port), the town reportedly was called Puerto Plata due to the silvery appearance of the surrounding mountains in the morning sun. With roughly 95,000 inhabitants Puerto Plata is a fairly large town with a distinctly Victorian architectural style due to the fact that many of the houses now standing were built between 1820 and 1920. These houses typically have the balconies, terraces and roof windows, as well as ornamental doors and windows, known as the *pan de ginebra* (gingerbread) style. The province of Puerto Plata produces sugar, coffee, cacao, tobacco, rum and dairy products.

To reach Puerto Plata from Santo Domingo follow directions for the Autopista Duarte and Santiago (Chapter 6) and then take the right turn for Puerto Plata, 14 km. (9 miles) after leaving Santiago. The easiest way to downtown Puerto Plata is to turn left at the first roundabout on the road from the west on Avenida Colon. Continue straight through town to the Malecon and turn left at the shore. The road ends at a large statue of General Gregorio Luperon on horseback (the man who restored Dominican independence by defeating the Spanish in 1864). Luperon was from Puerto Plata and he insisted on making this town the capital during his reign in the late 1870s. Santo Domingo became the capital again in 1880 when Luperon's hand-picked successor, Archbishop Fernando Arturo Merino, became head of state. To the left of the statue is the Fortaleza San Felipe which the Spaniards built in 1564–1577 to defend the town against English and French pirates. There is an RD$10 entrance fee to the museum which contains 16th century coins, tools, weapons, cannons and cannonballs. Visitors can climb the ram-parts and the fort affords a fine view of the port and nearby Mount Isabela de Torres. Throughout the centuries the fort has served as a jail and an arsenal for the different groups trying to secure their control over Puerto Plata. Juan Pablo Duarte (the Dominican George Washington) was even held prisoner in the fort for three days before being forced into exile in 1844. Rafael Trujillo used the fort to hold political prisoners as recently as the 1950s.

One of the most interesting places to visit in Puerto Plata is the Amber Museum (Calle Duarte 61, tel. 586-2848). To reach the museum from Fortaleza San Felipe, go down the Malecon for 6 blocks and turn right just after the impressive Victorian-style red and white building labeled *"Bomberos"* (firemen). The street you will then be on is called Calle Emilio Prud'Homme. Continue for 8 blocks until you see the sign for the Amber Museum on the right at the intersection with Duarte. The museum is on the second floor of a picturesque Victorian mansion. At the museum entrance is a pleasant rooftop area complete with benches and a good view of the city. The first floor has a good quality tourist shop where amber and other Dominican goods can be purchased and in back is a cafe. The museum is open Mon. to Sat., 9am to 5pm (tel. 809-586-2848), and admission costs RD$10.

Dominican amber is derived from the sap of a now extinct tree (probably related to pine) which grew extensively in this part of the world roughly 20 to 40 million years ago. Prehistoric insects and plant fragments caught in the sticky sap have been immortalized. Dominican amber is mined in shale/sandstone sediments on the north coast in the most extensive deposits in the world (rich deposits are also found in the Baltic region). Dominican amber is valued for its transparency and wide range of color, including blue, red, white, yellow and black. The museum's amber collection includes these different colors as well as pieces with various insects and even lizard eggs. There is also raw, or unpolished amber to demonstrate what it looks like freshly mined.

Upon leaving the museum you can either take Avenida Duarte (the road in front of the museum) to the left (west) to get back to Avenida Colon or go back the way you came to the Malecon. Puerto Plata is an old city with many narrow streets which lead nowhere so it is easier to stay on the main roads. Two blocks down Calle Duarte is Independence Park on the right with a fine old gazebo built in 1880. Several reasonably priced local restaurants surround the square.

Another enjoyable place to visit in Puerto Plata is the Isabela de Torres Nature Reserve, a small mountain (782 meters, 2565 ft.) just to the south of Puerto Plata. The *teleferico*, the only cable car in the Caribbean, takes visitors to the summit where they can see an impressive Christ figure similar to the statue overlooking Rio De Janeiro in Brazil. Alternatively, a horseback ride up the mountain is possible. The 22 square kms. (8.5 square miles) of the park encompass the mountain and include a botanical garden. Several birds visit the park, including the palm chat, Hispaniolan woodpecker, honeycreeper, common ground dove, Hispaniolan parrot, plain pigeon, limpkin, and red-tailed hawk.

To reach the teleferico drive up Avenida Colon away from the ocean to the roundabout. Turn right (west) and continue for .8 km (.5 miles) until a main paved road on your left goes up hill. There is a sign but it may be obscured by foliage. It costs RD$10 for a round trip ticket and each car takes about 20 people. Cable cars are supposed to leave every 10 minutes, but in practice it seems more like every 20 minutes. There are snack bars both at the summit and at the base of the mountain.

Another attraction in Puerto Plata is the Brugal rum factory on Avenida Luis Ginebra. Rum is a major Dominican product and a visit to this bottling plant is an enjoyable experience. To reach the rum factory from the teleferico continue back to the roundabout on Avenida Colon, proceed straight ahead on Avenida Circunvalacion past the park by Avenida Isabela de Torres, and then turn left on Avenida 27 de Agosto and right on Avenida Luis Ginebra (a major road), where the rum factory is located on the left. Visitors entering Puerto Plata from Sosua or the international airport should take the right fork at the roundabout where Avenida Luis Ginebra and Avenida Circunvalacion diverge. The rum factory is on the right side. Enter through the main gate and follow the guard's instructions. There are English-speaking tour guides waiting to explain the entire rum making process and to offer free samples at the end of the tour (Mon. to Fri., 9–12 and 2–5 pm).

Good beaches near Puerto Plata include: Guarapito (to the west and shaded), Cofresi (named after a 17th century French pirate, located to the east) and Long Beach near town and frequented by the locals. To the east of town about 12 km. (7 miles) on the road to Sosua is the Puerto Plata International Airport.

Playa Dorada

Playa Dorada is perhaps the most famous and most popular resort area on the north coast. Located about 6.4 km. (4 miles) east of Puerto Plata, it is a collection of 10 first class hotels (see Appendix) and more than 20 restaurants along a well maintained 24 km. (15 mile) stretch of carefully managed beach front. There are an excellent golf course designed by Robert Trent Jones and an active nightlife with classy discos, nightclubs and casinos. Playa Dorada is a fully self-contained area where well heeled visitors can get everything they want.

Sosua

Located 21 km. (13 miles) east of Playa Dorada is Sosua (18,800 inhabitants), founded in May of 1940 by German Jews fleeing the Nazis. In an effort to improve his international image, Dominican dictator Rafael Trujillo offered in 1938 to admit

100,000 Jewish refugees from Europe. Trujillo contributed a 26,000 acre tract on the north coast at Sosua and more than 800 settlers eventually arrived. Although many settlers found it difficult to adapt to rural Sosua and eventually made their way to the United States, some well educated settlers remained and developed an agricultural community based on milk and meat products. This town has a much more European flavor than most places in the Dominican Republic, especially the El Batey area where most hotels are located. Two distinct parts of town, El Batey and Los Charamicos, are separated by the long Sosua beach. Fortunately no road runs along this beach so visitors can enjoy the spot without the sound of motor vehicles. Shopping for souvenirs is easy with roughly 200 small shops selling everything from T-shirts and food to jewelry or scuba diving lessons. Los Charamicos contains strikingly poorer neighborhoods than El Batey, although ironically El Batey was the 18th century name for the areas where the slaves lived.

Besides enjoying the beach, there is much to do in Sosua. Signs in German are everywhere in El Batey, but the reason is the current popularity of the town with German tourists rather than the fact that German was spoken by the town's founders. Prices are not bargain basement, but hotels and restaurants are generally much cheaper than the luxury resorts in Playa Dorada and service tends to be good. To enter El Batey from the main road, turn left (if coming east from Puerto Plata) on Calle Duarte across from Los Almendros Hotel. Bear right at the fork (the left is one way against you), cross one street (Calle Pedro Clisante), and turn left on Alejo Martinez as you pass a small triangular park on the right. On the right is a sign for Koch's Guest House, a good deal and one of the original (German-owned) Sosua hotels. To the left Sosua Hotel is also recommended. Reasonably priced hotels abound in El Batey (see Appendix). For those arriving by yacht, the boat club is on the other side of the beach in Los Charamicos (tel. 535-6168) about a block further along the coast.

To reach the beach from El Batey, simply go back to Pedro

Clisante (one block over from and parallel to the main road), turn right and then turn left a block later at the taxi stand. A popular glass bottom boat ride is available on the *Dominican Queen*, 40 minutes for RD$75.

An impressive synagogue built by the Jewish refugees is located in El Batey on Calle Alejo Martinez across from the telephone company office and next to Sea Breeze restaurant. The caretaker is usually willing to show the synagogue to interested visitors. Next door is Industria Lecheria, the prosperous milk products company established by the original Jewish immigrants.

Another Sosua option is the Sandcastle (tel. 571-2420), an all-inclusive luxury hotel located along the beach in the Puerto Chiquito complex northwest of Los Charamicos. Besides ready access to a fairly uncrowded public beach, the Sandcastle resort hotel has two large swimming pools, a number of good restaurants, several shops and generally good service.

Cabarete

Cabarete is a mecca for windsurfers due to strong winds and stable currents. Located 13 km. (8 miles) further east than Sosua, Cabarete is a small town which offers several European style hotels (see Appendix) and restaurants. The establishments are generally concentrated near the center of town along the beach and people staying in town can reach everywhere on foot. Cabarete is popular with athletic young tourists and hosts a world class windsurfing competition.

Rio San Juan

Rio San Juan (12,800 inhabitants) is 64 km. (40 miles) east of Sosua and has yet to receive much attention as an international tourist resort. Two reasonably good hotels in this small village are: Rio San Juan and La Bahia Blanca. From the main coastal road going east (from Sosua) turn left on a paved road by the Texaco station. There is a sign at the turnoff for the Gri

Gri Lagoon (but not for the town). Hotel Rio San Juan is on the right along this street. This hotel has a clean and pleasant ambience, serves good (not cheap) food and has a large swimming pool. Windows on the rooms are not screened and mosquitoes can occasionally be a problem if the air-conditioners do not work well.

To reach Gri Gri Lagoon continue straight to the end of the main road. At this point is a boat rental area where boats can be hired for RD$200 by groups of less than 11 people (RD$20 extra for each person after the first ten). The boat trip takes an hour to ninety minutes and goes through Gri Gri Lagoon out into open ocean by way of a small island, the Cave of the Swallows (Cueva de Las Golandrinas) and Playa Caleton. The trip costs another RD$100 if the passengers decide to stop and swim. The boats appear to be in good condition and well maintained, but do not carry life jackets. These boats are not covered and visitors are advised to take adequate precautions against the sun.

To reach Hotel Bahia Blanca (the other good hotel in town), take the main road past Hotel Rio San Juan to the end (where the boats are), and turn left then bear right and follow the blue sign to the right to Hotel Bahia Blanca. This clean and comfortable hotel is located right on the beach and enjoys a constant ocean breeze.

Playa Grande

A superb beach 5.5 miles (8.8 km) east of Rio San Juan is known as Playa Grande and is popular with both Dominicans and foreign tourists. Visitors can drive to the beach and park without having to pay an entrance fee or go through a hotel. Palm trees near the ocean provide shade and the beach is bordered with pictuesque rock formations. Elaborate plans have been made to build a tourist complex similar to Playa Dorada on the western side on Playa Grande, but these hotels are not yet in place.

CHAPTER 5

Samana Peninsula

Samana peninsula is one of the most unique and popular places to visit in the Dominican Republic. Most of the original settlers were Americans—freed slaves in the 1820s—and English is still spoken by many local people. From here the visitor can take whale watching trips in the months of mid-December to mid-April. The three major areas of interest in Samana are Las Terrenas, Santa Barbara de Samana and Las Galeras.

History of Samana

Samana is unique within the Dominican Republic because many of its earliest settlers were Americans, freed slaves who arrived from the northern United States in the early 19th century. The entire island of Hispaniola was ruled by Haiti from 1822 through 1844. In 1822 Jean Pierre Boyer, president of Haiti, sent representatives to meet with abolitionist groups in New York and Philadelphia. Boyer wanted to attract black American settlers with farming experience to help secure Haiti's control over the remote Samana peninsula. The first American settlers, numbering about a thousand people, arrived in 1824 and suffered an epidemic of typhoid fever. Several hundred families of devout Methodists survived and became permanent residents of the Samana peninsula. Today their descendants still can communicate in fully comprehensible (although unique) English and number about three thousand. All are Dominican citizens and speak fluent Spanish.

In the 1850s there was great interest among rival U.S., British, French and Spanish interests in leasing or annexing Samana Bay to use as a naval refueling station. In 1854 a U.S. naval officer named Captain George C. McClellan outraged the Dominican authorities by taking the U.S. naval ship *Constitution* into Samana bay to investigate possible sites for a coaling station without even bothering to inform them. A draft treaty incorporating the Dominican Republic into the United States contained a clause that, in the event it was not ratified by the U.S. Senate, Samana bay would be leased by the United States. In 1869 the Grant administration sent two gunboats to Samana where, with the support of the English-speaking populace, a rally in support of U.S. annexation was held. Following the vote of the U.S. Senate in 1870 not to annex the Dominican Republic, however, U.S. interest in Samana declined and plans for a base in Samana were shelved. Over time English-speaking Protestants were gradually outnumbered by other Dominicans and are currently only about five percent of the population in the province. Despite attempts by Trujillo to suppress the use of English in Samana, its use has persisted among descendants of the American settlers.

Access to Samana

An airstrip just outside Las Terranas, across from El Portillo Beach Club, enables domestic flights to come in from Herrera Airport in Santo Domingo and other parts of the country. Another local airport is 11 km. (7 miles) west of the town of Samana along the paved road to Sanchez. It is also possible to arrive by boat from Sabana de la Mar to the south, but these small boats can only take passengers, not vehicles.

To reach Samana by car from Santo Domingo, take Avenida

John F. Kennedy west and continue as it becomes the Autopista Duarte going north to Santiago. About 16 km. (10 miles) out of downtown Santo Domingo is a toll booth (the only one on the route) which assesses RD$.50. Another 42 km. (26 miles) past the toll booth is the town of Piedra Blanca and the (unmarked) turnoff for Samana. Piedra Blanca is not well marked (there is a small sign on the left) and it is advisable to keep track of the distance. On the right side of the main road are a white cement pole and two buildings, Casa Valdez and Ferreteria Valdez. Turn right just across from the Esso station and continue on a narrower paved road.

The next town is Maimon (8 km., 5 miles further down the road) where getting lost is a real possibility. Turn right shortly after coming into town onto a street called Calle Sanchez, which is next to and across from green buildings painted with large 7up signs. Ask directions for Cotui, if there is any confusion about where to turn. The road is excellent for the next 13 km. (8 miles) until it passes Rosario Dominicana (the country's huge gold mine) on the left. During the time of the Taino, Cotui was already known for its gold. The Spaniards caught on quickly and in 1533 it was reportedly the second largest town on the island. Cotui is 30 km. (19 miles) along the road from Maimon and is fairly large (103,000 inhabitants) with several gas stations and unpretentious local restaurants. At the town square turn right, pass the church on the right and continue for three blocks until arriving at an Esso station with a sign indicating a half left turn for Pimentel.

Continue toward Pimentel by taking a right fork (which is unmarked) just 2.5 km. (1.6 miles) out of Cotui. The 14 km. (9 miles) distance between Cotui and Pimentel (18,000 inhabitants) passes through the Rio Yuna plain, the country's main rice producing area. To get through to Samana, turn right one block down from the Pimentel police station by a blue building labeled "Almacen Hernandez" and then take the next left by another blue building labeled "Almacen Aquino." Continue straight to the end of town and then make a right turn onto the major paved road. This excellent road goes through Castillo (Texaco station and 21,000 inhabitants) and 13 km. (8 miles) past Pimentel and then reaches the coast at Nagua.

Alternatively travelers arriving by car from Santo Domingo can stay on the Autopista Duarte all the way to the turnoff for San Francisco de Macoris and take that highway east through Pimentel to Nagua.

Nagua (64,000 inhabitants) is 59 km. (37 miles) from Cotui on an excellent road running along the north coast. (Beware of farmers using the edges of the road to dry beans and seeds.) At the edge of town there is a large green sign indicating a right turn for Sanchez, the first town on the Samana peninsula. Take this right and the next (unmarked) right fork. The road offers a pleasant view to the left as it meanders along the shore. Just 8 km. (5 miles) out of Nagua on the left is Hotel Carib-Caban (tel. 543-6420), an Austrian managed hotel/restaurant serving excellent food. Another 29 km. (18 miles) down the road is Sanchez, a fishing and trading town of roughly 24,000 inhabitants, but the town is of no particular interest to most foreign tourists. To by-pass the town bear left and continue on the main paved road.

The left turn (marked) for Las Terrenas is 35 km. (22 miles) from Nagua just past a Texaco station. The next 14 km. (9 miles) to Las Terrenas are up a steep slope from the south edge of the peninsula over the central mountains and down to the north coast. The road is in excellent shape (fortunately) although the Dominicans have not built the sort of scenic overlooks the area deserves. The panoramic view of Samana bay, the peninsula and the mainland to the south is arguably the best on the island.

Las Terrenas

Upon entering the remote town of Las Terrenas the traveler will realize that the Europeans have landed—recently. An abundance of modern, well-run hotels follow the coast and are filled with sun-seeking northerners. The first popular beach area is to the left at Punta Bonita where there are four good hotels right on a gorgeous little bay. Follow signs for Punta Bonita and Atlantis Hotel and proceed about 1.6 km. (1 mile) down a dirt/sand road to the ocean and then turn left. The hotels are Hotel Acaya, Punta Bonita Beach Hotel, Atlantis and Punta Bonita Cabanas.

Proceeding from the main street of Las Terrenas the next left leads to even more extensive tourist resorts along the beach. Along the sand road are about a dozen good quality beach hotels generally managed and patronized by Europeans (and occasional Canadians) including: Cacao Beach Resort, Hotel Las Cayenas, La Louisiana, Hotel Tropical Banana, Isla Bonita Hotel & Restaurant and La Hacienda.

Las Terrenas is the only sizable town (6,000 inhabitants) on the Atlantic coast of Samana peninsula. Continuing out of town and east along the coast for about 4 km. (2.5 miles) the traveler comes to El Portillo Beach Club across from the very small airport. This hotel, like many of the best Dominican hotels, takes the inclusive (American plan) approach under which a flat fee covers all meals and activities so that guests do not need to think about every transaction during their vacations. El Portillo Beach Club is situated right on a beach with a reef and provides snorkel gear. Sports such as volleyball, tennis, and horseback-riding are all included, as are merengue dancing lessons and nightly entertainment. The hotel is located in a remote area where guests can walk undisturbed for miles along the beach. Motorbikes can be rented ($8/hour, $33/day) to explore the surrounding countryside. Horseback riding trips in the remote countryside can be arranged at El Portillo Beach Club.

Near the hotel entrance is the Goga Nova art gallery with attractive paintings, wood carvings and local handicrafts for sale. Archeologists have discovered extensive ruins of Taino settlements in this area. Tourists should beware of unscrupulous locals who take genuine Taino pottery fragments and incorporate them into new pottery which is sold as if it were original.

The road east along the coast from El Portillo via Limon to

the town of Samana is very rough. Unless the traveler has a four-wheel drive vehicle with high suspension and lots of time, it is more sensible to return to the main road via Sanchez and take the southern road to Samana. For travelers taking the rough road east, it is possible to stop and rent horses and guides (prices negotiable) from local people. One enjoyable 6 km. (4 mile) side trip by foot or horseback is the Salto (waterfall) de Caloda just past Limon (about 10.5 km., 6.5 miles east from El Portillo). After about 30 km. (19 miles) the rough road reaches Samana after passing some beautiful scenery and remote areas.

Santa Barbara de Samana

Santa Barbara de Samana is on the south coast of the peninsula and can be reached by continuing straight (not turning north to Las Terrenas) when driving east past Sanchez. There are lots of potholes for the first 13 km. (8 miles) after which the road improves. The Samana airport is on the left 18 km. (11 miles) down the road from Sanchez and Samana town is 29 km. (18 miles) from Sanchez.

The town has 43,200 people and is laid out along the bay with the main street (the Malecon) and most popular restaurants along the waterfront. The town was founded by the Spanish in 1756 and settled with immigrants from the Canary Islands to secure the area from attacks by French buccaneers. On the western edge of town overlooking the bay is the Cayacoa Beach Hotel with its long pedestrian bridge extending half way across the bay to the small island of Cayo Vigia. The deepest part of the bay is roughly 45 meters deep. Cayacoa Beach Hotel can be reached by taking a right at the first roundabout as you come into town by way of Sanchez. Continue up the hill until the hotel is on the left; to the right the road leads to Puerto Escondido, a pleasant little beach just 400 meters (¼ mile) down the hill. The hotel has 66 double rooms, 2 suites and 6 cabanas, as well as a restaurant and a swimming pool. To use the pedestrian bridge over the bay, enter the Cayacoa Beach parking lot, walk out through the back gate and then down the path (there is no charge and the bridge is open to the public). It takes about half an hour to walk all the way out to the end of the last island. The solid concrete walkway is in reasonably good shape and the view is worth the effort. In the bay to the left of the walkway there are usually many yachts from France, Canada, the Netherlands, Britain and the United States.

Nightlife is active in Samana and is concentrated along the waterfront. On the ocean side of the street are a number of informal outdoor stands selling food and drink, largely to a Dominican clientele who sit on benches talking, listening to music and hanging out. On the opposite side are a number of restaurants catering to foreigners and more affluent Dominicans in roughly equal proportions. One of the best is Cafe de Paris which serves food (breakfast, lunch and dinner) as well as drinks and ice cream (closed Monday). Other outdoor restaurants along this strip include El Restaurante de la France, La Mata Rosada (with a shallow pool containing several turtles), El Camilo, El Nautico and on the ocean side next to the pier El Bucanero (offering live music and a bar). One restaurant with a good view of the bay is the Chinese restaurant Boite located on top of a hill overlooking the town within easy walking distance of the main street (easy to see from below). Further down the main street on the eastern edge of town is the Tropical Lodge.

Most of the original town was rebuilt in the 1960s to encourage tourism. Fortunately the old Protestant church, *la churcha*, was left standing. To find it, start down the main street going east (as if you were just arriving from Sanchez) and take the first left on Duarte. Proceeding up Duarte you see the large Catholic church on the left with its distinctive separate bell tower and the Protestant church slightly further up the hill on the right side of the street. The Protestant church dates from 1823 and is still in use by a bilingual congregation.

Boats can be rented at the main pier in Samana to Los Haitises National Park (Chapter 9) or Sabana de la Mar just on the other side of the bay.

Whale Watching

Humpback whales migrate along the north coast of the Dominican Republic each year from mid-December through mid-March. The whales come from areas near Newfoundland, Nova Scotia, Iceland, Maine, Massachusetts and Greenland to mate in warmer waters. Humpbacks do not eat during their three month visit to the Caribbean; they are here strictly to breed. Pregnant females have a 11- to 12-month gestation period before giving birth to a one-ton fetus which consumes 50 gallons of milk each day. Mature humpbacks are often 12 meters (50 feet) long and weigh 30 to 40 tons. These whales do not actually have humped backs—the name comes from the fact that they arch their backs as they dive. The whales can often be seen "flying" out of the water for a couple of minutes above the surface (breaching). These acrobatics are performed by male humpbacks courting fertile females. The 40-ton mammals move quickly and catching them in photos is not easy. Seeing these creatures in their natural habitat is exhilarating and well worth the effort for travelers who don't get seasick and visit during the right time of year. Boat rentals can be arranged in Samana for groups of 25–30 people and leave fairly early in the morning. One person who arranges whale watching trips and can be reached in Samana via the Tropical Lodge or Gran Bahia is Kim Beddell. Beware of going out in small boats with local people to see the whales. Some inexperienced local operators have not stayed far enough away from the whales in the past and people have drowned.

Even more popular with the whales than Samana is Banco de la Plata (Silver Bank), which is an underwater sanctuary located 64 km. (40 miles) north of Samana. Banco de la Plata has an average depth of about 20 meters and covers 3,748 square km.

(1,447 miles). Shallow water makes the area hazardous for navigation by large boats (which has helped to protect the area). This sanctuary was created by the Dominican government in 1986 with international support to protect humpback whales. Scientists estimate that between 2,000 and 3,000 whales visit each winter, roughly 80 percent of the humpback whale population in the north Atlantic. Humpbacks tend to prefer relatively shallow water close to islands, a preference which in the past made them vulnerable to human predators.

Cayo Levantado

A favorite day trip for visitors to Samana is an excursion to the island of Cayo Levantado for a relaxing romp in the sun and surf. Several boats take people over to the island for RD$50 round trip from the town's main pier. A typical trip departs at 10:30 am and returns about 4pm. In the larger boats the trip out to the island only takes about half an hour. White sandy beaches and lush vegetation cover the 2 km. by .5 km. extent of the island. No motor vehicles are on the island and the ambiance is very relaxing. Dominican food and drink vendors are on the island in abundance and meals can easily be obtained. Fresh lobster is readily available. The island is very popular with young European tourists who generally come in groups and some visitors report that the island sometimes gets too crowded. People seeking secluded areas can usually find them by walking for fifteen minutes or so past a complex of abandoned buildings to the far side of the island. A gentle breeze always caresses the island so visitors do not become overheated. No hotels are currently operating on the island but Occidental Hotels plans to open one in the not too distant future.

Las Galeras

Perhaps the most idyllic spot on the peninsula is Las Galeras to the north on Rincon Bay. Fortunately a paved road from Samana reaches all the way to Las Galeras and goes past beautiful sea-scapes. Take the road in Samana along the waterfront (the Malecon) north past the Yacht Club to the end of town, up the hill and turn right at the intersection at the sign for Las Galeras. Down the road 8 km. (5 miles) on the right is a boat yard where small boats can be rented for somewhat less than in town to go out to Cayo Levantado, Sabana de la Mar or the Parque Nacional de los Haitises. Gran Bahia is a large Victorian-style luxury hotel complex along the coast 10.5 km. (6.6 miles) north of Samana just across from Cayo Levantado. Adjacent to Gran Bahia is the Playa de Flechas (beach of arrows) where Columbus landed on January 12, 1493, at the end of his first voyage. The name Playa de Flechas is derived from the Europeans' first encounter with hostile natives. However, some historians claim this battle took place further north near Las Galeras at Playa Rincon. Today Playa Rincon is a beautiful beach well worth a visit but it requires a high clearance vehicle with four-wheel drive.

The paved road north ends at the small navy post in Las Galeras, 29 km. (18 miles) from Samana. This area has a distinctively Gallic ambiance with topless French women often wandering along the white sandy beach. The Moorea Beach Hotel is a pleasant place to stay in a quiet and relaxed setting. Local vendors wander along the beach but are subdued and easy-going. The Dominican naval presence guarantees security but is not obtrusive. Taino artifacts, fresh lobsters and beer are readily available. Nearby are two quality establishments, Restaurant Martinique and the Jardin Tropical Bar Restaurant. Visitors can walk along the undeveloped beach for miles to the east.

CHAPTER 6

The Cibao

Cibao is a Taino word for *plain*. The Cibao region encompasses the large central valley in the northern third of the country and the surrounding hills.

Santo Cerro

The Santo Cerro (Holy Hill) is situated on the southern edge of the Cibao valley and symbolizes a very important point in the history of Hispaniola. On March 25, 1495, Christopher Columbus planted a tall cross on the crest of this hill and proceeded to inflict a major defeat on a group of hostile (heathen) natives. According to a very old legend, the Virgin Mary appeared above the cross and ensured victory to the Spanish Christians. In the Church of Our Lady of Mercy (Nuestra Senora de las Mercedes) at the top of the hill, is the spot where the cross was put into the ground, the Santo Hoyo de la Cruz. As a sign of modern attitudes, a type-written note next to an old painting of the battle explains that the Virgin "was not against the Indians who were also her children, but through the Santo Cerro she has been venerated since antiquity and many people have come to God." The present-day church was built in 1880 using bricks from the ruins of La Vega Vieja (see below). Outside the church is a beautiful view of the Cibao valley and a pleasant courtyard. Nearby shops sell religious materials and a small church museum commemorates significant events in the development of the local church. Every year on March 25 a pilgrimage to this site is carried out by thousands of Dominican faithful.

To reach Santo Cerro drive north on the Autopista Duarte from Santo Domingo toward Santiago until arriving in La Vega (north of the turnoff for Constanza). Take the right fork on the major (paved) road toward Moca. There is an Isla gas station in the middle of the fork and the turnoff has a sign for Moca. Continue north 5 km. (3 miles) to the well-marked turnoff on the left. Proceed up the hill past 17 religious statues along the 1.6 km. (1 mile) road. Turn left at the top of the hill and the road ends at the church.

Ruins of La Vega Vieja

Continue north on the road to Moca from Santo Cerro for another 2 km. (1.3 miles) until arriving at the (turnoff marked) ruins of the Franciscan Monastery. With the completion of the monastery in 1512, La Vega became the seat of the first archbishopric on the island. Its foundations have been excavated and a footbridge has been erected over the site for easy viewing. A number of very old skeletons are arranged around the site, protected by tin roofing, and local people will be glad to point them out.

Up the road 1 km. (.6 miles) to the north are the ruins of the Fortaleza de la Concepcion on the left. Columbus built this fortress in 1495 following his decisive victory over the Indians of Santo Cerro. This site is of major archeological importance and has been a rich source of information about the original Spanish settlement of the island. In 1498 the fort withstood a major Indian attack and by 1503 La Vega was one of the largest towns in the Americas. The town grew rapidly in 1505–10 spurred largely by the discovery of local gold deposits. By about 1516 the gold deposits were depleted and in 1562 the town itself was destroyed by a major earthquake. La Vega was then rebuilt at its current location.

Recent excavations at La Vega Vieja have uncovered an extensive network of walls, rooms and passageways which enable archeologists to reconstruct a sense of what life was like for these early settlers. In back of the ruins is a museum containing a rich supply of Spanish and Indian artifacts from daily life, as well as various religious articles taken from the Franciscan Convent. This small museum in the midst of the ruins gives the visitor a glimpse of how the early Spanish colonists lived.

Moca and the Road North

A pleasant alternative route to the north coast (instead of Autopista Duarte via Santiago) is a scenic (and paved) country road running through Moca and eventually reaching the north coast at the town of Saboneta de Yaisca, not far from Sosua. To take this route turn off from Autopista Duarte and follow the directions (above) to Santo Cerro. Then continue north on the paved road for 11 km. (7 miles) to Moca. Moca is a fairly large town where the traveler should exercise care not to lose the road north. Entering town from the south there is a small triangular park on the right side of the road with a peculiar statue of a half column which honors the assassin of a former Dominican head of state. On July 25, 1899, the ruthless dictator Ulises Heureaux was murdered by Ramon Caceres while on a visit to Moca.

Continuing past the park the road leads to the Church of the Sacred Heart (La Iglesia del Corazon Sagrado) on the left side. The church has impressive stained glass windows and is quite large. Continue straight along the same road (Angelo Morales) through town until reaching Duarte, a large cross street with a median. Turn right here and take the next left on Jose Rodriguez. One block further is a sign on the right side for Salcedo and San Francisco de Macoris (straight) or Santiago (left). To continue to the north coast take the left fork toward Santiago, proceed for 3 km. (2 miles) and then take the right (marked) turn for Jamao.

The paved road from here to the coast has little traffic, frequent curves and great scenery. Take the (marked) right turn to Jamao 5 km. (3 miles) out of Moca. A pleasant little resaurant La Cumbre (the summit) lies 13 km. (8 miles) out of Moca along the right side of the road. With a fantastic view of the entire Cibao valley this clean and inexpensive restaurant is a good place to stop for a snack. The road passes through Jamao and joins the road along the coast 43 km. (27 miles) north of Moca at Saboneta de Yasica. Turn left (west) for Sosua or right (east) for Samana or Rio San Juan.

San Francisco de Macoris

The town of San Francisco de Macoris (population 165,000) has gained a great deal of notoriety over the last few years for its alleged links with the drug trade in New York City. A significant number of Dominican immigrants from this part of the Cibao are said to be involved in selling drugs as "foot soldiers of the Colombians" on the streets of New York. Many individuals have become incredibly wealthy; many others have disappeared. However, these Dominicans reportedly become law-abiding citizens when they return to the Dominican Republic and tourists are not bothered in San Francisco de Macoris. San Francisco does not have any particularly interesting tourist attractions, but is on the main road from Santiago to Nagua and the Samana peninsula.

Santiago de Los Caballeros

Santiago is a large city and driving through without getting lost may prove difficult. With more than 490,000 inhabitants, this city is the second largest in the country. Visitors driving in from the northwest (e.g., from Puerto Plata or Monte Cristi) come into town on Avenida Salvador Estrella Sadhala. Continue on this road all the way downtown (roughly 6 km., 4 miles) until coming to a large statue of Juan Pablo Duarte facing to the right in the center of a traffic roundabout. Continue straight for another 3 blocks and turn left at the roundabout (marked by an unnamed man on horseback facing left and a Rotary Club symbol) onto Autopista Duarte. Santo Domingo is roughly 145 km. (90 miles) from Santiago on the fairly busy but fast moving Autopista Duarte.

Santiago de los Caballeros was originally founded by Barthlomew Columbus and thirty of his knights (los caballeros) in 1495. The original city was completely destroyed by an earthquake in 1562 and that site is now known as Pueblo Viejo. In 1660 the French pirate Fernando de la Flor raided the Cibao valley from Puerto Plata and sacked Santiago. A census in 1737 found only 500 Spanish inhabitants. However by the beginning of the 19th century a resurgence in agricultural exports, especially tobacco, raised the population to roughly 27,000. Even today tobacco remains extremely important in the Cibao with small scale farmers raising the crop to be made into hand rolled cigars which are said to be as good as those from Cuba. Santiago is also an important center for lumber, mining, agriculture, rum distilling, coffee and sugar processing, livestock raising and manufacturing. Carnivals are held in February and August. According to popular belief, merengue music originated in Santiago.

Approaching Santiago on the Autopista Duarte from the south, the traveler sees an impressive white marble structure 66 meters (200 feet) high, the Monument to the Restoration of the Republic. This monument is surrounded by a sizeable park and is a popular place for local people to hang out. The monument affords an excellent view of the city and the Cibao valley. Adjacent to the park on the north side is Hotel Matun (see Appendix). Another alternative is the Hotel Santiago Camino Real, probably the best hotel in town. The Camino Real has a good restaurant (El Hidalgo) on the sixth floor with a wonderful panoramic view of the city. The hotel is located on Calle del Sol at the corner of Mella Avenue and has a popular discotheque on the premises.

The center of the city is Duarte Park with a charming pavilion dating from the turn of the century. On one side is the Catedral de Santiago Apostol, an imposing 19th century building combining Gothic with neoclassical elements and a fairly modern exterior. Not far from the cathedral at the intersection of Calles 30 de Marzo and 16 de Agosto is the Tobacco Museum where cigar making is demonstrated. Tobacco is a very important crop in the Cibao valley and this island was the place where European people were first introduced to the drug nicotine. A good tourist shopping area is not far from the park along the Calle del Sol. Cockfights can be seen in the Gallera Municipal on the road to Tamboril on the eastern edge of the city.

San Jose de Las Matas

Less than an hour's drive to the west of Santiago is the mountain town of San Jose de las Matas. To reach San Jose proceed as if returning to Santo Domingo and then turn right at the intersection with the statue of a man on horseback and the Rotary Club wheel (instead of continuing straight). Continue straight through a roundabout and across the Yaque del Norte River on a new bridge. Shortly after crossing the river turn left on a perpendicular road west toward Janico (26 km., 16 miles) and San Jose (40 km., 25 miles). The road curves quite a bit but the scenery is impressive.

With only 68,000 residents, San Jose de las Matas is a pleasant mountain town surrounded by pine trees. The people are more European in their appearance than people in most other parts of the country, which is probably attributable to early settlement by large numbers of Spanish farmers in the fertile Cibao area. Upon entering town a sign points to the Hotel La Mansion and the Parque Touristico to the right. The hotel's name comes from the fact that Trujillo maintained a mansion for his personal use in San Jose. The hotel is a large and comfortable structure up on a hill overlooking town. Arguably the best bargain in the country, the hotel provides a luxurious atmosphere for a reasonable price. Food and service in the restaurant are good. Although the hotel still belongs to the Dominican government, it is being managed by Occidental Hotels. Horses are available for rides into the surrounding countryside. The hotel has 22 large and comfortable double rooms and 100 villas nearby, as well as a large swimming pool and two outdoor whirlpools.

Mata Grande and the Trail to Pico Duarte

The road from Santiago passes through a small town called Pedregal 3 km. (2 miles) before arriving in San Jose. Travelers interested in hiking through the Armando Bermudez National Park to Pico Duarte from the north should turn left here. A paved road continues for another 10 km. (6 miles) passing some beautiful weekend houses and great scenery. Continue straight on the main dirt road for another 14 km. (8.5 miles) to Mata Grande. Here there is a park rangers' office where a permit to climb Pico Duarte (the highest mountain in the Caribbean) can be obtained for RD$50 (see Chapter 10) and local people with mules can be hired as guides. Note: The climb to Pico Duarte is at least 2 days longer from this starting point than from La Cienaga. If two cars are available, hikers might consider starting here and ending at La Cienaga or Saboneta.

CHAPTER 7

Southwest Coast and the Central Border Region

This region is the part of the country least touched by tourism. Much of the area is a sparsely populated, desert region with few tourist hotels. However, important attractions such as national parks and vast undeveloped coasts exist and prices for the services available are not high.

Leaving Santo Domingo take Avenida George Washington (El Malecon) west along the ocean toward San Cristobal. Along the Malecon past Ciudad Ganadera where the road turns away from the shore notice the monument on the left at the spot where Trujillo was assassinated on May 30, 1961 (see Chapter 3). The white concrete monument commemorating the assassination was constructed in 1981. Driving 4 km. (2.5 miles) further you will pass through a toll (RD$.5) and the road to the main port of Haina on your left. San Cristobal is 13 km. (8 miles) further along this heavily traveled road. A good paved road runs all the way to Barahona, but finding the way through the towns along the way can be difficult.

San Cristobal

San Cristobal is the birthplace of former dictator Rafael Trujillo who ruled the country from 1930 until his assassination in 1961. The town has roughly 138,000 inhabitants and is 30 km. (19 miles) west of Santo Domingo along the coast. There are interesting houses with a distinctively small town ambiance. On the edge of town Trujillo had a palace, Casa de Caoba (Mahogany House), which is gradually being restored by the government as a tourist attraction. To visit the Casa de Caoba or the La Toma baths turn right (north) on Avenida Constitution just past the town square and continue straight for 2.7 km. (1.7 miles) out of town through the Nigua River valley. Eventually an intersection appears with a sign indicating that La Toma is to the right. Turn here and continue for another .8 km. (.5 miles) to a sign for Casa de Caoba on the left. Through the gate and another .8 km. (.5 miles) uphill is the palace with an impressive view of the surrounding countryside. This excursion is a good way to see a bit of the Dominican countryside and the road is paved except for the last .8 km. (.5 miles).

Coming into San Cristobal from the east the road crosses the Nigua River and comes immediately to a roundabout. On the far side of the roundabout is Hotel Terraza (RD$120/night). Bear right and then take the first left at the sign indicating Bani ahead. Two blocks further is the town square on the left. Good beaches near San Cristobal are Najayo (where the ruins of one of Trujillo's houses still stands), Nigua, and Palenque.

To reach Barahona and points west, continue straight; to visit the baths of La Toma turn right at the end of the square on Avenida Constitucion. The road to Bani and Barahona continues past a crowded local market on the right (also known as

Mercado Modelo). Further along on the right is an army base and in this area are *policia acostado* (sleeping police) or man-made ridges in the road which must be crossed slowly. The army base houses the local jail for both men and women. Continue straight on this road to leave town heading west.

To reach Balneario La Toma continue on the same road for another 3.4 km. (1.5 miles), roughly 6.4 km. (4 miles) from town, until the entrance appears on the left. The La Toma baths are an extensive series of connecting pools fed by an under-ground spring. The area has plenty of shade trees, ample parking and a restaurant complex alongside the pools. La Toma has slides and shallow pools for children as well as plenty of larger pools for adults. The pools and restaurant are privately operated by Efrain Lucas (tel. 528-2995) and charge a modest RD$20/adult and RD$5/children. La Toma is open Mon–Fri 9am–6pm and Sat–Sun 7am–8pm. Food and drink are available. The clientele are generally local people and visiting La Toma gives the traveler the opportunity to encounter Dominicans at play.

Inexpensive local hotels in San Cristobal include: San Cristo-bal, Constitution (just past the turnoff for La Toma and Casa de Caoba), El Calminante and Wing Kit.

Bani

The next major town to the west (another 32km., 20 miles) is Bani with roughly 106,000 inhabitants. The Taino word *bani* meant "abundance of water." The town is notable mainly as the birthplace of Maximo Gomez (a leader in the 19th century strug-gle for Cuban independence from Spain) and for its municipal museum. The museum is in the large gray and white building on the western side of the town square and is closed on Sundays. The building doubles as city hall and is labeled "Palacio del Ayuntamiento." On November 21 Bani celebrates the day of the

Virgin of Regla. Not far from Bani are Los Almendros beach and the town of Palmar de Ocoa, noted for its fishing tournaments.

San Jose de Ocoa

About 18 km. (11 miles) further along the main road west from Bani is the River Ocoa and the turnoff for San Jose de Ocoa, a remote town with 67,000 inhabitants located 25 km. (16 miles) north in the mountains. The road into town is paved but (despite what the map may indicate) primitive roads north from town are steep and should not be attempted without a sturdy four-wheel drive vehicle. Although foreigners do not frequent the town, one reasonably good place to stay is Rancho Francisco which has 10 rooms and inexpensive cabins. Guests can use a swimming pool fed by the Ocoa River. The Rancho Francisco is located just south of town on the right side of the main road. Another inexpensive local option is Hotel Elias.

Azua

From the junction on the main road west the next major town is Azua (48km., 30 miles west of Bani) with roughly 87,000 inhabitants. Pueblo Viejo, the old city of Azua located 10 km. (6 miles) south of the present town, was founded in 1504 by Diego de Velasquez who later conquered Cuba. Hernando Cortes lived in Azua before conquering Mexico. Azua was one of the first Spanish colonial towns to suffer repeatedly from pirate attacks and the town's sugar mill was burned down in 1538. Following both a major earthquake and a flood in 1751, the inhabitants decided to rebuild the town in its current location. Azua is in a desert region and relies on irrigation to produce its famous watermelons and cantaloupes. The last Tainos were resettled in this area and a monument to the Taino leader Enriquillo (see Lago Enriquillo below) can be seen on the eastern edge of town along the road. A couple of good nearby beaches are Playa Chiquita and Monte Rio.

After leaving Azua the road continues through a very dry part of the country. This area is basically unpopulated outside Azua for at least the next 48 km. (30 miles) until the road arrives at the Yaque del Sur river valley. The turnoff for San Juan de la Maguana is 16 km. (10 miles) past Azua on the right and travelers heading for Lago Enriquillo or Haiti should continue straight (instead of right) at this point.

Barahona

Barahona (80 kilometers, 50 miles west of Azua) is a pleasant seaside town with 80,000 inhabitants where food and lodging can be had at reasonable rates. Probably the best hotel in town is the Guarocuya along the beach on the western edge of town. Hotel Guarocuya serves reasonably good meals and costs relatively little and visitors can swim at the beach. The plumbing is not great but guests are provided with potable water and most rooms have balconies looking out over the bay. Light sleepers should avoid rooms near the disco. Reservations are possible and the hotel occasionally fills up. Note: The hotel does not have its own electric generator; most rooms are not fully screened and mosquitoes can be bothersome if there is no city power. Across the street is Hotel Caribe with smaller rooms for about the same price and an effective electric generator which may make it preferable. Hotel Caribe also boasts a good outdoor restaurant, La Rocca. To find the Guarocuya and Caribe hotels when coming into town from the east, drive straight down to the waterfront and turn right on Avenida Enriquillo. Continue for about three blocks until there is a sign for Guarocuya on the left and a circular driveway down to the water. A good restaurant is Brisas del Mar located on the waterfront toward the east of town.

An excellent paved road built in 1991 runs from Barahona south along the coast through Paraiso, Enriquillo and Oviedo all the way to Pedernales on the Haitian border. There is a Swiss Hotel 10 km. (6 miles) south of Barahona which rents out budget rooms and camping spaces right along the ocean. Plans are being made to build other tourist facilities in this part of the country, but it has not happened yet. Accommodations for travelers are few and far between, although a new hotel is under construction in the town of Paraiso (Hotel Paraiso). The road passes beautiful seascape with small fishing villages before reaching Oviedo where it turns west away from the ocean.

Jaragua National Park

The Jaragua National Park office is in El Cajuil along the main road just east of Oviedo. The park is a huge (1400 square km., 541 square miles) undeveloped nature reserve stretching along the road to the coast and including the Beata and Alto Velo islands. Near El Cajuil is Lago Oveido, a large lake which is home to many species of birds including the country's largest population of flamingos. At the time of writing visitors must obtain advance permission to visit the park in Santo Domingo (see Chapter 1) and must be accompanied by local guides so that the delicate local flora will be protected. Trails are unmarked and facilities are limited to the main park office and three outlying ranger stations at Trudille, Fondo de Paradise and Bahia de la Aguila. The park staff is kept busy keeping track of dozens of poor local people, primarily fishermen, who live in the park in small settlements such as Trudille. To reach Trudille and Fondo de Paradise continue 10 km. (6 miles) west past the park office to the small town of Los Tres Charmicos and turn left at the park sign. Visitors with a high clearance four-wheel drive vehicle can drive the next 9 km. (5 miles) to Fondo de Paradise and then hike on a rough but spectacular trail for another 4 hours to the picturesque little fishing village of Trudille. With permission to visit the park, visitors can stay in the rustic facilities provided by the park service.

The average temperature is 27°C (81° F) and average annual rainfall is 500–700 millimeters (20–28 inches). High temperatures and low rainfall have favored the growth of cacti. Besides flamingos other birds in the park are the great egret, little blue heron, sooty tern, American frigate bird, roseato spoonbill, white-crowned pigeon, black-crowned palm tanager and green-tailed warbler. The ricard and rhinoceros iguanas, both native to Hispaniola, can be seen at the park. Hawksbill, leatherback, loggerhead and green marine turtles also live in the area. The park's name comes from the name of a Taino kingdom and the park contains numerous traces of the Taino dating back as far as 2590 BC. The park contains ancient caves, such as Guanal, La Cueva la Poza and Cueva Mango, which contain Taino petroglyphs.

Pedernales

Another 32 km. (20 miles) down the road from Los Tres Charmicos is a paved turnoff for Cabo Rojo on the left where the Alcoa Company once mined bauxite and where small scale limestone mining continues. Just 600 meters past the Cabo Rojo turnoff on the right is the marked turnoff for Al Acetillar Nature Reserve, the southern extremity of the Sierra de Baoruco National Park. Visitors with a high clearance four-wheel drive vehicle can drive all the way through to Puerto Escondido (see Sierra de Baoruco). Another 13 km. (8 miles) along the main road is Pedernales, a fishing village straddling the Haitian border at the mouth of the Pedernales River. Tourist hotels and restaurants have not yet reached the town, although there are a couple of rustic local places: Hotel Noruega and Pension Familiar Hungria. Many small fishing boats (but no pier) line the water's edge and cross-border smuggling is said to be common. No paved road crosses into Haiti at Pedernales and vehicular traffic across the border into Haiti is not permitted without special permission from the Dominican government. On the northwest edge of town the International Highway (which is actually a crude dirt track) straddles the Haitian border and leads to Sierra de Bao-ruco. However, travel along this remote route is potentially hazardous and should not be attempted by visitors unless they are accompanied by Dominican government personnel.

Lago Enriquillo

To reach Jimani or Lago Enriquillo from the east take the road toward Barahona and turn right roughly 50 km. (31 miles) past Azua at the sign for Vicente Noble. This road heads west to Neiba and along the north shore of Lago Enriquillo to Jimani.

Lago Enriquillo is the largest (265 square km., 102 square miles) lake in the Caribbean. This salt water lake is also the lowest point on Hispaniola at 40 meters (131 feet) below sea level. In ancient times the Bay of Neiba (Barahona) was connected to the Bay of Port-Au-Prince. The area gets extremely hot (35°C, 95°F) and receives very little rain. Lago Enriquillo provides sanctuary for crocodiles (best seen in morning), iguanas, turtles and flamingos. Roughly two-thirds of the way along the northern shore of Lago Enriquillo (before arriving in La Descu-bierta) is a sign on the right side for Las Caritas (the faces). There is no parking lot but it should be possible to pull over along the road and get out for a look. Near the top of the cliff to the right are numerous Taino petrogylphs which resemble faces and were made hundreds of years ago. Visitors can climb up the rocks for a closer look—at first the carvings are difficult to see from the road. There is a great view of Lago Enriquillo from the drawings. Unfortunately the carvings are not effectively protected and some have been defaced.

The lake derives the name Enriquillo from a famous Indian leader who rebelled against Spanish rule. As the son of a cacique killed by the Spaniards, Enriquillo was raised by friars at the Monastery of Saint Francis in Santo Domingo. Enriquillo, like other natives of that era, was required to work as a virtual slave on a Spanish encomienda. In the 1520s Enriquillo rebelled, fleeing to the remote Sierra Baoruco mountains with a band of followers. Enriquillo and his men successfully resisted capture by the Spaniards for years. The natives carefully followed the practice of disarming and releasing their pursuers, rather than killing them. Eventually the Spanish king sent a personal emissary to arrange a peaceful coexistence and negotiations were held on the Isla Cabritos in the center of what is now Lago Enriquillo. The Spanish crown granted Enriquillo his own fiefdom in the Baoruco mountains in return for his acknowledgment of Spanish rule.

About 1.6 km. (1 mile) past Las Caritas on the left is a parking area for Isla Cabritos (Goats' Island) National Park. This uninhabited island in Lago Enriquillo was declared a national park in 1974 and is well worth a visit. Usually an amiable National Park employee in uniform is available to show visitors the local flora and fauna along the edge of the lake, including the huge iguanas native to the area. Sulphur baths are available here. To visit Isla Cabritos, visitors must make advance arrangements with the Ecoturista office in Santo Domingo. Ask for Elaine Velasquez (tel. 221-4104/06, fax 689-3703). The office is located near the male obelisk along the Malecon in the Eugenio Maria de Hostos Park (Vicini Burgos street). Visitors to the Isla Cabrito National Park should rent a boat (for RD$500) and obtain permits for each person (RD$50 for foreigners, RD$20 for Dominicans) at this office. There are two motor boats operated by the park authority that go out to the island regularly. Trips are possible seven days a week and mornings are the best time to visit; there is a three-person per group minimum. National Park officials accompany visitors to the island, taking them to a small museum and then on a hike to the southern side of the island where crocodiles can be observed in their natural habitat. Tips are appreciated.

Isla Cabritos is only 12 km. (7 miles) long and 2.5 km. (1.5 miles) wide with no fresh water on the island. American crocodiles as well as ricord and rhinoceras iguanas (all of which are listed as endangered species) roam the island. Visitors should beware of the relatively numerous population of scorpions (which are poisonous but generally not lethal). The island's interesting flora, such as neoabottia treecactus, harrisia, cayuco cactus, alpargata cactus, cholla cactus, common lignumvitae, ziziphus, catalpa and mesquite, are able to live in the high temperatures with very little water. Birds found on the island include flamingo, great blue heron, Louisiana heron, black-crowned heron, least bittern, glossy ibis, purple gallinula, burrowing owl, roseatte spoonbill, Hispaniolan parrot, white-crowned pigeon, West Indian nighthawk, and the village weaver (which was introduced from Africa).

About 3 km. (2 miles) down the road is La Descubierta where visitors can visit the local balneario and swim (without crocodiles). Travelers returning to Santo Domingo can avoid retracing their paths by continuing around the southern side of Lago Enriquillo (counter clockwise). Continue straight past the statue of Enriquillo at the Mella junction and turn left on the main road north from Barahona. This route passes the Laguna de Rincon, a 47-square km. (18 square miles) science reserve which contains the largest fresh water lagoon in the country, on the left. The reserve is home for fresh water shrimp and Hispaniolan fresh water slider turtles as well as the masked duck, ruddy duck, flamingo, Louisiana heron, glossy ibis, blue-winged teal, sora crake, and Northern jacana.

Jimani

The only two places where travelers can cross officially from the Dominican Republic to Haiti by land are Dajabon in the north (see Chapter 3) and Jimani (8,500 inhabitants) in the south. Under the terms of a long-standing treaty between Haiti and the Dominican Republic, private cars can stay for thirty days. Unfortunately, some travelers report bureaucratic delays as well as requests for bribes by border officials (particularly on the Haitian side) when crossing the border by car. The main land route between the two countries is an excellent paved road from Santo Domingo along the coast and west past Lago Enriquillo to the Dominican border at Jimani. The road on the Haitian side from Jimani to Port Au Prince is passable, but is not fully paved and requires crossing some difficult areas. In Jimani travelers headed to Malpasse, Haiti, will find primitive lodgings, greasy restaurants, and money changers. Colorful Haitian buses go both ways and can carry budget travelers.

Sierra de Bahoruco National Park

South of Jimani and Lago Enriquillo is the Sierra de Bahoruco National Park which stretches for 800 square km. (309 square miles) in a remote, pine covered mountain area along the Haitian border. To reach the park go to Duverge on the road along the south side of Lago Enriquillo, 40 km. past Jimani to the east. From Duverge take the dirt road on the southwest edge of town into the mountains toward Puerto Escondido which is 11 km. away. Driving into Puerto Escondido take the first right and look for the flag to find the national park office.

From Puerto Escondido there are two ways to enter the park by vehicle. The rough (high clearance four-wheel drive required) road to the left (north) leads to Loma de los Pinos through the heart of the park and eventually to El Acetillar (see Pedernales). Alternatively to reach Loma del Torro (the highest peak in the park at 2367 m., 7764 ft.) and the area along the Haitian border take the main road west (very rough road, high clearance vehicle is needed) past the military post El Aguacate (19 km., 12 miles away) to the unmarked trail on the left to Loma del Torro (34 km., 20 miles from Puerto Escondido). Note: It is unwise to continue along the road down from the mountain from Loma del Torro to the border unless accompanied by Dominican government personnel. Both high peak areas of the park have pleasant trails passing a rich variety of flora.

As noted above, the Sierra de Baoruco was where Enriquillo chose to fight the Spaniards in 1532 and ultimately received his fiefdom. Today the park provides an important sanctuary for birds such as the Antillean siskin, La Selle's thrush, chattanger, narrow-billed tody, white-winged warbler, Hispaniolan trogon, Antillean elaenia, white-crowned pigeon, red-necked pigeon, white-winged dove, Hispaniola parakeet, Hispaniola lizard cuckoo, Hispaniola parrot, palm crow, sparrow hawk, common bobwhite, vervain hummingbird, broad-billed tody, stolid fly-catcher, great Antillean pewee, rufous-throated solitaire and the white-necked crow which is extinct in Puerto Rico and can only be seen on Hispaniola.

Cabral

The town of Cabral is 20 km. (12 miles) east of Duverge on the road to Barahona. A marked road south from Cabral leads to the nearby polo magnetico where a significant magnetic force has been caused by the geological make-up of the area. Visitors can test this natural phenomenon by driving with liquid in an open container—it will appear they are going up or down hill while the drive is actually level.

The park in the center of Cabral is painted blue. The road north past the park leads to the Laguna Rincon (also known as Laguna de Cabral), the largest fresh water lagoon in the country and home to the endemic Hispaniolan slider turtles. Birds in the area include the masked duck, ruddy duck, flamingo, Louisiana heron, glassy ibis, blue-winged teal, sora cake and northern jacana.

San Juan de la Maguana

To reach San Juan de la Maguana take the (marked) north fork 16 km. (10 miles) west of Azua. With 130,000 people, San Juan is a sizeable town which depends primarily on agriculture and cattle. The Maguana were one of the five original Taino states on the island in 1492. The town is named after San Juan El Bautista (St. John the Baptist) and the Maguana Indians. After passing through 64 km. (40 miles) of arid countryside from the turnoff near Azua, San Juan de la Maguana appears. Approaching from the west a distinctive arch marks the center of town. Hotel Maguana to the immediate right of the arch is a reasonably good hotel by local standards with an impressive structure dating from the Trujillo period. The dining room is reasonably good, rooms have screens and the pool is in working order. Alternatively, one block up the road is the cheap and rather dirty Hotel Tamarindo.

North of town is the somewhat mysterious Corral de los Indios, a reminder of the departed Taino. To reach the Corral, continue on the main road into town until you reach Anacaonda Street with a large sign for "Banco Popular Dominicano" and turn right. A statue of John the Baptist soon appears on the left. The Corral is another 5 km. (3 miles) along this road and is marked by a government sign, "Bienvenido al Corral de los Indios." This ancient Indian meeting ground is a large flat circle roughly 300 meters (328 yards) in diameter with stones arranged along the perimeter and in the center. The area has a beautiful view of the surrounding mountains. This spot may have been used for tribal meetings or, considering its flatness, for ball games.

The Dominican high peak region (La Cordillera Central) is not far away. A trail to Pico Duarte (see Chapter 10) originates by the Saboneta dam. To reach the Saboneta dam continue along the road for another 19 km. (12 miles) north from the Coral through Juan de Herrera along a rough road. At the dam local people know where to start the trail up Pico Duarte and where to rent mules.

A road runs west from San Juan de la Maguana to Comendador on the Haitian border. Pass military headquarters in San Juan on the left and continue straight out of town. The road turns to dirt and eventually arrives at a crossroads called Matay-aya. Here the main road continues straight to the Comendador, a sleepy little border town which used to be a major crossing point in the days of Trujillo. The largest building in town is a huge castle-like customs complex which was abandoned years ago. The border is closed to vehicular traffic at this point. Rustic hotels in town are Erania and Eureka. While the scenery in this area is impressive, travelers should be advised that facilities are non-existent, border controls are minimal and the area is best left to smugglers and the army. The only good road connecting the north and south coasts in the Dominican Republic is the Autopista Duarte running from Santo Domingo to Santiago and Puerto Plata.

CHAPTER 8

Santo Domingo

The capital city has roughly 2 million residents and sits along the Ozama River on the southern coast of Hispaniola. According to popular belief, Santo Domingo owes its present location to a 15th century plea bargain. Miguel Diaz, an early Spanish inhabitant of the settlement at La Isabela, fled the north coast settlement after having fought and wounded another settler. Diaz headed south into the wilderness and eventually ended up on the south coast romantically involved with an Indian maiden named Catalina. Catalina revealed to Diaz the location of the Indian gold mines on the banks of the Haina River not far from present-day Santo Domingo. Diaz traded this information for a full pardon from Bartholomew Columbus, Christopher's brother and governor of La Isabela. The Spanish moved south looking for gold and in 1496 Bartholomew Columbus founded the first Spanish settlement on the south coast along the east side of the Ozama river. Following a common 15th century practice, Christopher's brother Bartholomew Columbus named the new town to commemorate their father Domenico by choosing the name of his patron saint, Santo Domingo. The formal name of the town later became Santo Domingo de Guzman after Dominic de Guzman (1170–1221), the founder of the Dominican religious order.

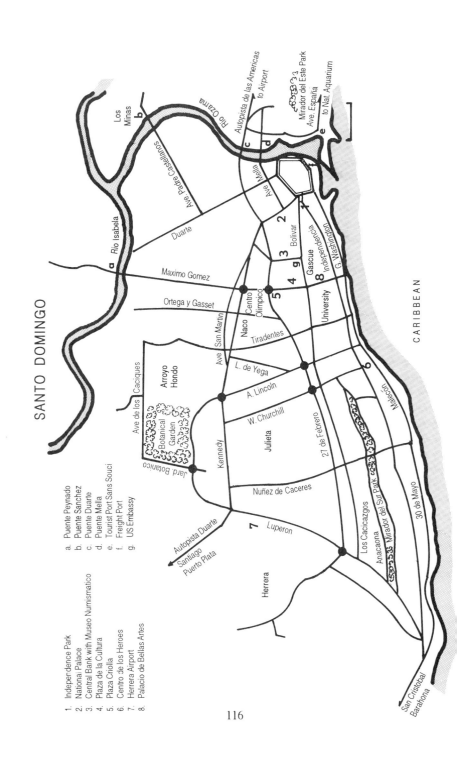

SANTO DOMINGO

1. Independence Park
2. National Palace
3. Central Bank with Museo Numismatico
4. Plaza de la Cultura
5. Plaza Criolla
6. Centro de los Heroes
7. Herrera Airport
8. Palacio de Bellas Artes

a. Puente Peynado
b. Puente Sanchez
c. Puente Duarte
d. Puente Mella
e. Tourist Port Sans Souci
f. Freight Port
g. US Embassy

CARIBBEAN

Originally the town was made of wood and destruction caused by the earthquake of 1502 prompted Nicholas de Ovando to rebuild the city in stone on the western side of the Ozama River. Santo Domingo was built with right-angled streets, making it easier to defend from both outsiders and internal uprisings. The success of Santo Domingo's city plan is evidenced by its use as a model throughout colonial Spanish America. Santo Domingo was founded during the late Middle Ages and was one of the last cities to be built with a city wall. Nicholas de Ovando started the wall along the river and the sea since attack by land was considered less likely. The entire wall with seven gates was completed by the middle of the 16th century and ran north from where nowadays the Malecon and Palo Hincado Street intersect at the Parque de la Independencia and then northwest on what is now Juan Isidro Perez Street to the Ozama River.

Over the years Santo Domingo has been subjected to natural and man-made forces which have dramatically altered its appearance. Earthquakes devastated the city in 1673, 1684, 1842 and most recently in 1946. Sir Francis Drake left the city in shambles in 1586. Hurricanes in 1930 and 1979 (David) wrought terrible destruction. Until the mid-19th century Santo Domingo remained a fairly small town and only after independence from Haiti in 1844 were residential areas outside the original city walls added. These new neighborhoods, such as Ciudad Nueva and San Carlos, were inhabited largely by immigrants from the overpopulated Canary islands.

The first systematic expansion of the city took place during the Trujillo years when various structures (described below) such as the National Palace, the Centro de los Heroes, the Altar de la Patria, the Palacio de Bellas Artes and the Malecon were built. Trujillo owned virtually all land west of the city as far as the Haina River and when he died that land was seized by the government and subdivided in modern neighborhoods such as Naco, Piantini, Los Prados, and El Millon (which were settled rapidly by people migrating in from the countryside). At the beginning of the Trujillo era in 1930 the city had barely 200,000 inhabitants. Thirty years later the population had doubled and by the mid 1970s more than a million people lived in Santo Domingo. During the last 15 years the population doubled again and is now about 2 million. City limits reach from the Haina River in the west, to the Isabela River in the north and almost as far as Boca Chica to the east.

Present-day Santo Domingo has expanded far beyond the original colonial zone. Unfortunately no beltway exists to avoid city traffic. The main east-west avenues (west of the Ozama River) are George Washington (the Malecon), 27 de Febrero, and John F. Kennedy. The three bridges over the Ozama are named after the three heroes of the independence struggle with Haiti: Sanchez, Duarte and Mella, with traffic flowing only west on Duarte Bridge (at the end of 27 de Febrero) and east on Mella Bridge from 6 to 9 am during work days. Traffic moving west can take Bolivar and San Martin; traffic going east can use Independencia. The main avenues running north-south are Maximo Gomez, Ortega y Gasset, Tiradentes, Abraham Lincoln, Winston Churchill, Nuñez de Cacares and Luperon (see map).

The Colonial Zone

The Zona Colonial (colonial zone) is the original Santo Domingo within the city wall and is the oldest continuously inhabited European settlement in the Americas. Today the colonial zone is a bustling commercial district with many places of interest. Although the colonial zone is not simply a museum, it is well endowed with numerous examples of early 16th century Spanish architecture. To see everything would be so time consuming that the most effective approach is to decide what is likely to interest you the most and spend your time accordingly. Visiting the colonial zone can be done many ways and numerous Dominican guides of varying reliability are eager to lead visitors around for a small tip. Alternatively, a walking tour is outlined here for those travelers deciding to see the main sights on their own.

Colonial Zone Walking Tour (see map and numbers)

To get to the colonial zone drive south from anywhere in Santo Domingo west of the Ozama River towards the ocean. The street running along the shore is George Washington Avenue, commonly known as the Malecon. Turn left (east) and proceed all the way to the large black statue facing the sea on the right and a little park with part of the city wall and two cannon on the left. The 33m. (110 ft) tall statue is of Antonio Montesino (1), an early 16th century Spanish defender of the Taino Indians. His ardent appeal for justice for the indigenous population was the first known call for human rights in the Americas and this statue was a gift from the Mexican government. From the second level of the statue there is a good view of the harbor. Before reaching the statue turn left by the blue restaurant on the corner called Restaurant La Bahia (on the corner of Calle 19 de Marzo across from the little park). Take the first right along the park (on Gabriel Garcia Street) and continue through two intersections past a little park on the right as the road takes a left turn. Take the first right (on Padre Billini Street) and continue for a block to Las Damas where the road ends and Fortaleza Ozama can be seen on the left. Parking in this area is generally not difficult.

Fortaleza Ozama (2), the oldest fortress in the Americas, was built in 1503–07 by Nicolas de Ovando to protect the settlement from pirates and British privateers. Upon entering the fortress walk toward the statue of Gonzalo Fernandez de Oviedo, a military historian of the new world and fortress commander from 1515 to 1525. Cannons overlook the nearby Ozama River where early settlers unloaded vital supplies from Spain and from the interior. The fortress and its 18 m. (55 ft) high tower, the Torre del Homenaje (3), are completely restored and provide a pleasant

Barahona

Caracas

Ave. Duarte

Calle Ravelo

Calle Felix Ruiz

Calle Benito Gonzalez

Calle Puello

Calle Gral. Cabral

Jacinto de la Concha

Calle Altagracia

Calle del Monte y Tejada

Calle Jose Reyes

Calle Restauracion

Calle Emiliano Tejera

Avenida Mella

Calle Santome

Calle Juan Perez

Calle Santiago Rodriguez

Calle Mercedes

Rio Ozama

Calle 16 de Agosto

Ave. 30 de Marzo

Ave. Bolivar

Calle General Luperon

Calle Jose Reyes

Calle Espaillat

El Conde

Calle Arzobispo Nouel

Calle Duarte

Calle Hostos

Calle Arzobispo Merino

Calle Isabella la Catolica

Calle Las Damas

Ave. Independencia

Calle Santome

Calle Padre Billini

Calle 19 de Marzo

Calle Arzobispo Portes

Calle Palo Hincado

Calle Sanchez

Calle Jose Gabriel Garcia

Paseo President Billini

Puerto Ozama

Calle El Numero

Calle Barahona

Calle Cambronal

Calle Carreras

19 20 21 22 23 24 25 26 27 28 29 30 31 32 33 34 35

1 2 3 4 5 6 7 8 9 10 11 12 13 14 15 16 17 18

COLONIAL ZONE

1. Statue of Antonio Montesino
2. Fortaleza Ozama
3. Torre de Homenaje
4. Casa de Bastidas
5. Casa de Cortes, (Maison de France)
6. Hostal de Nicolas de Ovando
7. Panteon Nacional
8. Casa de las Gargolas
9. Museo de las Casas Reales
10. Capilla Nuestra Señora de los Remedios
11. Sundial
12. Plaza de Maria de Toledo
13. Alcazar de Colon
14. Puerta de San Diego
15. Puerta de la Atarazana
16. Museo de la Atarazana
17. La Atarazana
18. Casa del Cordon
19. Duarte Museum
20. San Francisco Monastery
21. Hospital San Nicolas de Bari
22. Porcelain Museum
23. Convento de Regina Angelorum
24. Capilla de la Tercera Orden
25. El Convento de los Dominicanos
26. Parque Duarte
27. Casa Tostada
28. Plazoleta Padre Billini
29. Callejon de las Curas
30. Cathedral Santa Maria La Menor
31. Plaza de Colon
32. Independence Park
33. Puerta El Conde
34. Altar de la Patria
35. Mercado Modelo

respite from the bustling city. The Torre del Homenaje was often used to house prisoners, including Christopher Columbus' son Diego prior to his return to Spain in 1520. The tower's walls are 3 meters thick; it was used for political prisoners as recently as the 1950s by ruthless Dominican dictator Rafael Trujillo. More recently the fortress was occupied by police during the 1965 civil war and was heavily shelled by leftist insurgents. Explore the grounds and climb the tower to enjoy an excellent view of the city. Faro a Colon (Columbus lighthouse) and the huge government flour mill can be seen across the river. The fortress is open 8am–6pm on Mon. and Wed. to Sat., and 10am–4pm on Sun. Admission costs RD$4.

Leaving the front gate of the fortress, turn right and proceed down this quiet street, Calle de las Damas, on foot. Calle de las Damas was built in 1502 and is the oldest street in the hemisphere. When Diego Columbus was appointed governor in 1508, he arrived with an entourage of nobles and their wives. Every morning Diego's wife, Maria de Toledo (a niece of the Spanish king Ferdinand) walked with the noble wives down this street to Mass. Watch for a plaque on the right wall marking the Casa de Bastidas (4) with an 18th century stone sculpture of Santa Barbara on the roof above the gate. Inside of Casa de Bastidas is a spacious courtyard (open to the public 8am–6pm seven days a week) with Romanesque arches and benches shaded by several large rubber trees. On both sides of the courtyard are impressive art galleries. To the left of the entrance is a stylish artisan shop. The house was built in 1527 by Rodrigo de Bastidas who went on to govern Coro, Venezuela, and Santa Maria, Colombia.

On the left at the next corner (intersection with El Conde) is the Casa de Cortes (5), formerly occupied by Hernan Cortes the conqueror of Mexico. The house was built in Gothic style by Governor Ovando in 1503 and currently contains the Maison de France (the French Cultural Association). The Casa de Cortes is open to the public and displays art work from time to time. Continuing down Las Damas, the Hostal de Nicolas de Ovando

(6) is on the right. Historians do not know exactly where on the east bank of the Ozama Christopher Columbus lived when he governed Santo Domingo from September 1498 to October 1500. However, he definitely stayed in this building as a guest of Governor Ovando from August 13 to September 12, 1504. The Hostal de Nicolas de Ovando is a tastefully restored 16th century structure which combines the original home of the wealthy Davila family with Governor Ovando's official residence. The hotel's pool area marks the connection between the two originally separate houses. The hotel is highly recommended for comfort, good food and an old world ambiance in the heart of the colonial zone. On the left is the Panteón Nacional (7), formerly a Jesuit convent established in 1747. The National Pantheon contains the remains of such 19th century Dominican notables as General Pedro Santana, the man who temporarily cancelled independence and reunited the country with Spain. The Pantheon was restored in 1955 when dictator Rafael Trujillo constructed an ornate tomb for himself, one that he never was allowed to occupy. General Franco of Spain donated the magnificent bronze chandelier. After Trujillo's assassination in 1961, the Dominican government refused to inter him in the Pantheon and his remains were buried in Paris at the Pere Lachaise cemetery. Around the corner to the left from the Panteón Nacional is the Casa de Gargoyles (8) (currently the Dominican Development Foundation), where visitors can see gargoyles which were once on the cathedral to ward off evil spirits.

Leaving the Pantheon turn left and continue down Las Damas past Calle Mercedes until reaching the Museo de las Casas Reales (9) (Museum of the Royal Houses) marked by a huge anchor on the left at the next corner. The museum is the restored 16th century palace of the Spanish Governor's Royal Court and contains an excellent collection of royal artifacts including maps of sea voyages during the colonial period, paintings, restored court rooms, carriages, treasure recovered from 16th century Spanish ships, coats of armor, rifles, miniature ships and an elaborate model of the original walled settlement. President Balaguer and

King Juan Carlos I of Spain inaugurated the building in 1976. The museum is well maintained and worth the RD$10 entrance fee. Hours are Tues. to Sat., 9am–5pm, Sun. 10am–1pm, closed Monday. Across from the Museo de las Casas Reales is the small La Capilla de Nuestra Senora de los Remedios (10) built by Francisco Davila and used for Mass before the cathedral was constructed.

Upon leaving the museum turn left and walk to the end of Las Damas. Pass the sundial (11) built in 1753 and a row of cannons pointing out to sea on the right. Ahead and across the brick Plaza de Maria Toledo (12), a parade ground, is the rectangular, two-story Alcazar de Colon (13) (Castle of Columbus). Diego Columbus was appointed governor of Hispaniola three years after his father Christopher's death in 1506. Diego and his wife Maria de Toledo (King Ferdinand's niece) were accustomed to the elegant lifestyle of the Spanish court and were determined to live well in the humble new colony. The Alcazar palace was built from local coral rock in 1510–1514 and decorated with silk, velvet, precious wood, bronze and fine porcelain. The Alcazar contained 22 rooms, including a library and a music room, and was extravagant by the standards of the primitive 16th century colony. Diego was recalled to Spain in 1523, in part due to his reputation for self-indulgence, but his descendants occupied the Alcazar until the early 18th century. Widely considered one of the most splendid buildings in Spanish America, it was sacked by Sir Francis Drake in 1586. Trujillo undertook a major renovation of the Alcazar in 1955 although this restoration is generally believed to have paid scant attention to the design of the original structure. In 1971 the Balaguer government restored the building along the lines of its original construction.

The Alcazar is now an impressive museum depicting the life of the Spanish rulers at the time of Columbus. A fine collection of tapestries, old paintings, china, maps, religious icons, musical instruments and finely carved wooden furniture fills the Alcazar. The Spanish Renaissance style and open architectural design of the building and grounds are appealing. Notice the wooden ceiling beams with their intricately carved faces designed to ward off evil spirits. The building was built on the edge of the Ozama River to take maximum advantage of cool cross-breezes in the era before air-conditioning. Across the river are some of the most humble houses in Santo Domingo lining the water's edge. The Alcazar manages to convey an idea of daily life for the colony's 16th century elite and is well worth the admission fee of RD$10. Hours are Mon., Wed. to Fri. 9am–5pm, Sat. 9am–4pm, Sun. 9am–1pm, closed Tues. Tours are available in different languages. In back and to the right of the Alcazar as you face the river is the Puerta de San Diego (14) (Gate of St. James), where visitors can walk down to the river along the Avenida del Puerto. Parking is also available in designated places on the Avenida del Puerto near the Alcazar.

From the Alcazar proceed north along the city wall and down the steps to the Museo de las Ataranzas (16) (Shipyard Museum) directly across from the 17th century Ataranzas gate (15). This fascinating museum tells the story (in English and Spanish) of the early shipwrecks along the Dominican coast and various efforts to recover their treasures. Part of the exhibit displays artifacts recovered from the quicksilver galleons which sank during a hurricane off Samana bay in 1724. Gold used for personal adornment was not taxed by the Spanish government during that period and many passengers on sinking ships were weighed down by their own tax shelters. More than 400 shipwrecks, most of which have not been salvaged, lie buried off the island of Hispaniola. Museum hours are Mon. to Sat. (except Wed.) 9am–5pm, Sun. 9am–1pm (tel. 682-5834). After leaving the museum proceed around the corner to the right along La Ataranza street (17), built in 1503 as the first shopping center in the Americas. In colonial times the street was lined with an arsenal, the customs house, workshops and taverns. Nowadays the street contains several good art galleries, as well as restaurants and gift shops.

Continue up La Ataranza to the Palacio de Comunicaciones, a green building with a television tower on the corner of Emiliano Tejera Street. Walk up Emiliano Tejera and cross a street called Isabela la Catolica. On the left corner is the Casa del Cordon (18) (House of the Cord) built in 1502 by Francisco de Garay and allegedly the oldest stone building in the Americas. The building was named for the huge cord of the Franciscan Order sculpted above the entrance and is now occupied by the Banco Popular. The bank allows visitors to tour the building during normal business hours. Before moving into the Alcazar, Diego Columbus and Maria de Toledo lived in the Casa del Cordon and had two children there. This is also the spot where the women of Santo Domingo assembled before Sir Francis Drake in 1586 to surrender their jewelry as ransom for the city and its inhabitants.

Visitors will have an option to visit the birthplace of Juan Pablo Duarte when the historical museum occupying the spot reopens on February 27, 1992. Turn right at Casa de Cordon and proceed one block to 308 Isabela La Catolica street where the Duarte Museum (19) is on the left side. After visiting the museum return to Casa de Cordon.

From Casa de Cordon proceed two blocks up the hill on Emiliano Tejera street to the ruins of the San Francisco Monastery (20), on the right at the intersection with Hostos street. Built in 1508, this monastery was the first in the Americas. The monastery was built on a hill and the ruins consist of the church, the chapel of Maria de Toledo (Diego Columbus' wife) and the monastic grounds with large green areas visitors can wander around. The remains of Christopher's brother Bartholomew Columbus are reportedly buried on the site. The San Francisco Monastery was sacked by Drake in 1586 and destroyed twice by earthquakes in 1673 and 1751. In 1881 the monastery was converted into an insane asylum and chains used to confine inmates can still be seen. The ruins are being refurbished by the Jaycees and provide a pleasant resting point. Hours are 3:30pm–6pm Mon. to Sat. and Sun. 8am–6pm; no admission fee.

Leaving San Francisco Monastery turn right and walk down Hostos. Continue straight along Hostos on the high railed sidewalk as it heads downhill. This is not a wealthy area but the modest houses along the road are quite old and their classical architecture is pleasing. Cross Mercedes and continue past a church to the ruins of the Hospital de San Nicolas de Bari (21) on the left. The hospital, built by Nicolas de Ovando, 1503–1508, was the first stone hospital in the new world and probably one of the best constructed buildings of the period; the unrestored structure survived until 1911. Continue down Hostos and cross General Luperon. On the right is a great little restaurant/bar called Maison de Bari. This establishment is a favorite for local artists and businessmen, and serves good food in a relaxed (and informal) atmosphere.

Continue down Hostos one more block to El Conde, a modern pedestrian causeway with shops and galleries, and turn right. El Conde is a pleasant shopping arcade which extends all the way to Parque de la Independencia. Proceed three blocks along El Conde and turn left on Jose Reyes street. Cross Arzobispo Nouel Avenue and continue to the Porcelain Museum (6 Jose Reyes street), half way down the block on the right side. The Porcelain Museum (22) is located at 6 Calle Jose Reyes, between Avenidas Padre Billini and Arzobispo Nouel. The museum building was built at the turn of the century by the wealthy Vicini family, reportedly inspired by the Alhambra Palace in Spain. The museum contains a good porcelain collection, primarily of 18th and 19th century European pieces. Visitors can stop for a pleasant rest from the bustle of the city in the museum's back courtyard. A RD$ 10 contribution is suggested.

Proceed down Jose Reyes to Padre Billini street to El Convento de Regina Angelorum (23) (Queen of the Angels) at the intersection. Visiting the church and the tomb of Father Billini (who rediscovered the remains of Columbus in the cathedral in 1877 and worked to establish basic services for the poor) is possible by asking permission from the nuns who live within the complex. The church was built in 1537 and is a beautiful place with an intricate hand-carved mahogany altar in the Baroque style and fine silver grillwork backed by Moorish titles.

Two blocks further left (east) on Padre Billini avenue is the Capilla de la Tercera Orden (24) on the right side of the street, which was built by Dominicans in the 18th century and housed the first teaching seminary in the country. Next on the right side of Padre Billini is El Convento de Los Dominicanos (25), established in 1510. This church is believed to be the oldest standing church in the hemisphere and was the forum for Friar Antonio de Montesino's early 16th century speeches on behalf of human rights for the indigenous population. To enter the church take Hostos Street to the right and enter, by requesting permission, through the first door on the right in the old convent. The church is a beautiful place and visitors to Santo Domingo should not miss it. The main door on the west side of El Convento is decorated on the outside with distinctive 16th century tiles and is basically a late Gothic structure with decorative early Renaissance elements. Inside notice the Hapsburg eagle on the top of the Baroque altar, a gift from Hapsburg Emperor Charles V (Charles I of Spain), the grandson and heir of Ferdinand and Isabela. In the Rosary Chapel (to the right when facing the altar) astrological signs decorate the ceiling. The four seasons are represented by Jupiter, Mars, Saturn and Mercury revolving around the sun with the twelve signs of the zodiac (representing the twelve apostles) and the stars in the background. In 1538 the oldest university in the Americas, the University of St. Thomas Aquinas, was founded here and even today El Convento is affiliated with the Autonomous University of Santo Domingo. Across the street is Duarte Park (26) where the Indian princess Anacaona was allegedly hanged by Nicolas de Ovando in 1508 and where Sir Francis Drake hanged two uncooperative Catholic friars in 1586.

A block further on Padre Billini street at the intersection with Arzobispo Merino avenue is Casa de Tostada (27) on the right side. This early 16th century house was built in late Gothic style and houses the Museum of the 19th century Dominican family. The original owner was Francisco Tostada, the first person born on Hispaniola to become a university professor (at Thomas Aquinas). Tostada had the misfortune to be killed by Sir Francis Drake's men in 1586. The house has a unique Gothic double window on the second floor. The museum includes a good collection of 19th and 20th century Victorian wicker and mahogany furniture, a pleasant courtyard and an elegant terrace on the second floor. An excellent view of the city can be seen by climbing up the wooden spiral staircase. The museum is well worth the $RD10 admission and hours are 9am–2pm every day except Wed. From Casa de Tostada continue another half block down Padre Billini street and turn left into the picturesque alley known as Callejon de las Curas (29) (Alley of the Priests) where the cathedral's clergy live.

The 17th century Callejon de las Curas leads to the Geraldini (south) gate of the Catedral Basilica Menor de Santa Maria, Primada de America (30). This cathedral contained the remains of Christopher Columbus until they were transferred to the Faro a Colon (Columbus Lighthouse) on October 9, 1992. In 1542 Pope Paul III granted this cathedral primacy over all other churches in the Americas (as the name indicates). Although Diego Columbus set its first stone in place in 1514, the Spanish architect commissioned to build the cathedral went to Mexico and built a cathedral there rather than in Santo Domingo. Work finally resumed in 1521, financed largely by the Bastidas family, and the Santo Domingo cathedral was not completed until 1540. The bell tower remained unfinished due to lack of funds.

Largely as a result of the slow pace of construction and the involvement of different architects, the cathedral combines late Gothic vaults, a Renaissance facade and Romanesque arches. The Gate of Pardons (the north gate facing Plaza Colon) is the cathedral's only Gothic entrance. St. Peter's Gate (the main portal) has an impressive double arch and splendid ornaments above the two entrance doors. On both sides of these doors are niches which once contained bronze figures of St. Peter, St. Paul and four other apostles which were allegedly stolen by Sir Francis Drake. Beautiful stained glass windows were crafted by Rincon Mora, a Dominican artist. The cathedral has 14 different chapels and contains a number of medieval treasures. One is an anonymous painting, "Virgin de la Antigua", said to have been a gift from Ferdinand and Isabel of Spain brought to Santo Domingo by Christopher Columbus. This painting is on the left side when passing through the St. Peter's Gate. The main altar is carved from mahogany and houses a processional tabernacle made of silver which has been in use since 1542. There is a small relic taken from the cross of Santo Cerro (see Chapter 6) where the Virgin miraculously appeared to ensure victory to Columbus over the Tainos in 1495.

This 16th century cathedral has withstood earthquakes, hurricanes, foreign occupation and civil war for almost five centuries. The remains of Christopher Columbus were kept in a white marble and bronze memorial built by President Ulises Heareaux in 1898 but were transferred to the Faro a Colon on October 9, 1992. Nearby other dignitaries are buried, including Columbus' grandson Luis, his daughter-in-law Maria de Toledo and at one time his son Diego (although Diego's remains ended up in Havana, Chapter 3). In January of 1586 Sir Francis Drake made the cathedral his headquarters while plundering Santo Domingo and used St. Peter's chapel as a jail. Drake cut the nose and hand off a mahogany statue of Bishop Bastidas and stole the cathedral's bells. Despite the precedent of Drake's sacrilege, visitors are not currently allowed to wear shorts and miniskirts inside the cathedral.

Adjacent to the cathedral on the north side is the Plaza de Colon (31) (Columbus Plaza), a pleasant area with ceiba trees dominated by a large bronze statute of Christopher Columbus. Notice that the French sculptor, Gilbert, placed the Indian princess Anacaona at Columbus' feet in this 19th century statute. On the west side of the plaza is an intriguing neoclassical structure with a tower, known as El Vivaque, which was built in the 16th century and originally served as city hall. This building is currently occupied by the Banco de Trabajadores (Workers' Bank) and contains elaborate murals by Vela Zannetti which can be seen during business hours. On the opposite (east) side of the plaza is Palacio de Borgella, a two-storied white structure supported by two levels of brick arches. This palace was built by the Haitian governor Borgella in 1825 and served as the seat of government until 1947 when the National Palace was completed.

Parque de la Independencia

El Conde is a pedestrian causeway running through Santo Domingo's main commercial district from Calle de las Damas to Parque de la Independencia (32) (Independence Park). Santo Domingo was fortified in the mid-16th century with walls running along the Ozama river, the Malecon, Palo Hincado street and Juan Isidro Perez street. Independence Park is where the walls along what are now Palo Hincado and Juan Isidro Perez streets originally came together. The northern edge of Independence Park contains the ruins of La Concepción Fort which marks the northwestern corner of the original city wall and the end of the colonial zone. The 18th century Puerta El Conde (33) (Gate of the Count) was named after the Conde de Penalva who successfully defended the city against the British forces sent by Oliver Cromwell to conquer the island in 1655. This is where the Dominicans rose up against the Haitian garrison on February 27, 1844, and began their war of independence. In the center of the park is the Altar de la Patria (34) (Altar of the Nation) which was built in 1976 and contains huge statues (and the remains) of the three heroes of Dominican independence: Juan Pablo Duarte, Francisco del Rosario Sanchez and Ramon Matias Mella. Shorts and miniskirts cannot be worn into the mausoleum. This park is the center point for the country and all highway distance markers are supposed to be calculated from this point.

National Palace

The Palacio Nacional is a Renaissance-style castle built by Trujillo in 1947 and surrounded by 18,000 square meters

(21,528 square yards) of well landscaped grounds with a high fence. The palace is located between Dr. Delgado and 30 de Marzo Streets along Avenida Mexico. The palace, which was constructed using mahogany, Samana marble, gold and fine crystal, is a beautiful structure whose marble exterior varies from beige to pink depending on the sunlight. Unlike the U.S. White House, the National Palace contains the president's office but is not his home. Unfortunately the National Palace is not currently open to the public and only can be seen from the outside.

Mercado Modelo

For those travelers interested in visiting a bustling Third World market, Mercado Modelo is recommended. The market is housed in a huge two story structure on Mella Avenue near Santome Street. Parking in the immediate area is difficult and it may be necessary to walk a few blocks. Taxi drivers know how to get there. To reach the market from George Washington Avenue (El Malecon) drive east as though going to the colonial zone, turn left on Calle 19 de Marzo and continue straight for 4 blocks, then turn left on Calle Arzobisopo Nouel. Parking in this area is usually not difficult. Proceed on foot 3 blocks further to the corner of Calle Arzobispo Nouel and Calle Santome, and turn right on Santome. Go one block up Santome across El Conde (the pedestrian causeway) and continue four more (slightly uphill) blocks on Santome to Avenida Mella. Turn right and the entrance to Mercado Modelo is halfway up the block on the left. Note: This is a crowded area and it is not advisable to wear valuables, carry pocketbooks or bring cameras when walking through the streets to this market.

The entrance to the market is through a large arch up the wide stairs. The market is a maze of dozens and dozens of small shops where the owners (many of whom can speak at least some English) bargain over the price of their merchandise. The ritual involves feigning shock and disappointment when told the price of any object, and responding with a substantially lower offer. The seller will then react with disgust or dismay and start to put away the item, but will probably quote a slightly lower price along with a story about how much it costs to produce the item. Never pay the first price quoted and never offer to buy something and change your mind when the seller accepts your offer.

Hand-crafted products for sale include: wood carvings, decorative ceramics (including the faceless dolls from Neiba), jewelry made of larimar and amber (both of which the Dominican Republic is noted for), as well as semi-precious stones such as coral, colorful horned carnival masks, tambourines, drums, leather belts and saddles, wicker ware, pocketbooks, cigars, sandals, mahogany rocking chairs, tape cassettes of merengue music, T-shirts, and some impressive Haitian paintings. Certain stands sell voodoo potions and other mysterious concoctions, including love potions. On the second floor and around the fringes of the market meat and local produce are sold, mainly to Dominican customers.

The market is adjacent to Little Haiti, the Haitian section of Santo Domingo, and a considerable number of the merchants are Haitians. A lively cross-border trade with Port-au-Prince is conducted in brightly colored Haitian buses which leave every day carrying market women back and forth. These buses can be seen outside the back door of Mercado Modelo and over one block. Despite recent difficulties between the two governments, this cross-border trade is alive and well. It is possible to buy very inexpensive Haitian products, including straw mats and wood carvings, if you're willing to take the time to bargain and shop around. To reach an outdoor Haitian vegetable market turn left from the back door of Mercado Modelo and then left again. Conditions are quite basic and most customers are less affluent Dominicans, quite a contrast to shopping at a Giant or a Safeway in the states. This vegetable market is on Sansome, so continue straight to get back down to Arzobispo Nouel Street.

Plaza de la Cultura

The Plaza de la Cultura is a large park area (formerly Trujillo's property) bounded by Maximo Gomez Avenue, the U.S. Embassy, Nicholas Pension Avenue and Pedro Henriquez Urena Avenue on the north. To reach the Plaza de la Cultura from the Malecon, drive north on Maximo Gomez. One block up is the Palacio de Bellas Artes (Palace of Fine Arts) on the right where various exhibits and performances are held. Two blocks further is President Balaguer's residence on the right, next to the Papal Nunciature on the corner on Nicholas Pension, diagonally across from the U.S. consulate. Plaza de la Cultura is aptly named and contains the following important cultural centers.

Museum of the Dominican Man

The Museum of the Dominican Man contains fascinating anthropological information about the indigenous people, the African slaves and the Spanish conquerors. Dominican history, folklore and cultural development are described along with an interesting display of artifacts. There is a very good collection of costumes and carnival masks. The museum is well organized, stimulating and should be visited. Hours are Tues. to Sun., 9am–5pm.

Gallery of Modern Art

This impressive gallery is well worth the RD$10 admission charge. Four floors of modern art are arranged in a delightful and air-conditioned setting. Paintings by Dominican artists show the visitor a new dimension of this society that he might well not otherwise encounter. Elaborate sculptures, dramatic paintings and wood carvings and surrealistic photos fill the gallery. Jose Vela Zanetti, a Spanish artist whose murals grace the United Nations in New York, lived in the Dominican Republic and his huge murals convey a sense of the country to the viewer. Travelers who appreciate art will not be disappointed.

National Museum of Natural History

This museum contains various exhibits about the Dominican environment, including models of areas of particular geological interest, such as Lago Enriquillo. The evolution of plant and animal life on Hispaniola is displayed in detail, and the museum has a good amber collection. Considerable information is available about the local flora and fauna, including stuffed birds and animals which could make them easier to recognize in the wild. The museum is open Tues. to Sun. 10am–5pm.

National Museum of History and Geography

For travelers with an interest in history this museum provides a fascinating glimpse at the 1914–24 period of U.S. occupation, including photos and newspaper accounts of the U.S. soldiers (a rather undisciplined lot) and the Dominican resistance. An excellent collection of Trujillo memorabilia conveys a sense of the hardships suffered by the Dominican people during his dictatorship in 1929–61. The museum also has good coverage of the Haitian-Dominican battles of the 19th century, as well as the 1822–44 period of Haitian occupation. The entrance fee is RD$10 for foreigners and RD$2 for Dominicans.

National Theater

In front of the theater are statues of three giants from the golden age of Spanish literature: Calderon de la Barca, Tirso de Molina and Lope de Vega. The threater itself has a 1,600-seat capacity for opera, ballet and symphonic performances. The building was constructed in 1973 using native mahogany, marble and onyx. The National Theater has been the home to the national symphony orchestra since 1941. Concerts cost RD$30-150 and the ticket window is open 9:30am–12:30pm and 3:30pm–6:30pm. No jeans, tennis shoes or thongs are allowed at the National Theater, and men must wear socks. These rules don't apply to people under 15 years old.

National Library

The library contains a large and well organized collection of books in Spanish which can be read in the library without difficulty. The large, four floor structure includes ample space for visitors to sit and read.

Maniqui Restaurant

Located between the Gallery of Modern Art and the National Museum of Natural History, the Maniqui restaurant is quite good and reasonably priced. The choices actually available on any given day are often fewer than those listed on the menu. English is not spoken by the staff but the *plato tipico* is always a good bet. Maniqui is a place to relax and enjoy a meal, but not the place to go in a hurry.

National Botanical Gardens

In the northwest suburbs of Santo Domingo are the National Botanical Gardens where visitors can stroll through a vast area planted with all varieties of well tended tropical plants. To get to the gardens, drive north from the Malecon on Abraham Lincoln (by Hotel Santo Domingo) all the way up to John F. Kennedy Avenue where the road comes to a roundabout. Proceed across the roundabout where Abraham Lincoln becomes Avenida de los Proceres and continue to the next roundabout (with a seated statue of Jose Marti facing in the opposite direction) and turn right on Avenida Jardin Botanico. The entrance to the gardens is just ahead on the right.

The gardens cover more than 2.5 million square meters (618 acres) and give visitors the opportunity to see the rich variety of plants native to Hispaniola. The park contains shaded walks, decorative pools, fountains, benches and excellent vistas. There are enjoyable spots for a stroll and picnic areas, such as the Japanese Garden, the Great Glen, the Orchid Greenhouse, and the Bromelia Pavilion. The gardens include tropical vegetation, a palm forest, aquatic plants and more than 300 types of Dominican orchids. The entrance fee is RD$10 (for another RD$10 at the entrance tours in Spanish and English by miniature train are available of the entire area). Horse drawn carriages also take visitors for rides around the gardens. At the left of the main entrance is a large scale model of the gardens for those intending to walk around on their own. The gardens are generally not crowded and are open Tues. to Sun. 9am–6pm.

Zoo *(Parque Zoologico)*

Santo Domingo is fortunate to have a very good zoo. Unlike in many Third World zoos, the animals appear to be well taken care of and healthy. The zoo covers 1.5 million square meters (371 acres) and is well designed to maximize the area available for the animals yet retain safe vistas close enough for visitors to get a good view. The African-like tropical climate is ideal for many of the zoo's residents, such as the zebras, lions, leopards, tigers, camels, hippopotami, rhinos, antelope, hyenas, mountain goats, monkeys, ostriches, turtles and crocodiles to roam about in semi-freedom. Pink flamingos, native to the area, are free to come and go as they please. Monkeys and colorful birds (including 30 different kinds of parrots) move around energetically in large cages.

The zoo is open seven days a week from 9am to 6pm and costs RD$5 for adults and RD$3 for children, plus RD$2 for parking. The enjoyable 15-minute train ride costs only RD$5 per person. To reach the zoo from the Botanical Gardens (see above) turn right on Avenida Jardin Botanico upon leaving and take the second right on Avenida de los Caciques. This street becomes Paseo de los Reyes Catolicos and leads to the zoo.

El Malecon

The Malecon, officially known as George Washington Avenue, is the seafront boulevard which periodically becomes the world's largest open air disco. The Malecon extends along the waterfront from the statue of Friar Anton de Montesino on the edge of the colonial zone all the way to the spot where Trujillo was assassinated on May 30, 1961, on the road to San Cristobal. Tall Royal palm trees line the Malecon, a major commuter artery. More than sixty hotels, bars and restaurants line the Malecon and virtually every evening after 11 pm a party atmosphere reigns. Three of the city's best hotels, the Jaragua, Sheraton and Santo Domingo, are on the Malecon. The carnival and merengue festivals are centered along the Malecon and take place on February 27 and the last week in July respectively.

Carnival originated in medieval Europe as a big party just prior to forty days of austerity during Lent. The celebrations in Santo Domingo have been embellished with African elements and are as exuberant as the more well known celebrations in Rio de Janeiro and New Orleans. Hundreds of wooden stall *casetas* are set up along the Malecon to sell rum, soft drinks, beer, sandwiches, fruit and snacks, and each *caseta* is equipped with a radio. The carnival celebrations build to a climax on February 27, Independence Day. A parade begins in late afternoon with the arrival of the newly elected king and queen of the celebrations, followed by floats and marchers from various municipalities, businesses and clubs. Local people dress in a bewildering array of costumes, including the *diablo cojuelo*, a horned devil who lashes out at bystanders with inflated cows bladders to purge them of their sins. Anthropologists connected with the Museo del Hombre Dominicano have traced this devil to medieval Europe. Fascinating costumes whose designs are very much of African origin can be seen worn on the marchers. Hundreds of thousands of spectators line the Malecon during the parade and local television does complete coverage. The celebration continues all night long with euphoric dancing, singing and partying in the street all along the Malecon.

The merengue festival in the last week of July also takes place along the Malecon and involves all night dancing and partying.

Thousands of tourists from Puerto Rico and Western Europe come to participate.

Several important developments in Dominican history are reflected along the Malecon. Two obelisks built by Trujillo have a special significance. The smaller one (at the intersection with Palo Hincado street) looks like a huge tuning fork and was built in 1942. Known as the female obelisk, it was built to commemorate Trujillo's success in repaying the Dominican foreign debt and regaining control over Dominican customs from the United States. The second obelisk at President Vicini Burgos street was built in 1955 at the peak of Trujillo's power to celebrate changing the capital's name from Santo Domingo to Trujillo City. Heading east on the Malecon (toward the colonial zone) the building just past Santo Domingo Hotel on the left is the old Ramfis estate, the former home of dictator Trujillo and currently the Foreign Relations Ministry. The area west of Winston Churchill avenue along the Malecon is called La Feria and was the site of Trujillo's 1955 World's Fair of Peace and Brotherhood. The impressive buildings Trujillo built for the fair currently house the Supreme Court, the Congress, the Attorney General's Office, the Department of Agriculture and City Hall. At the heart of La Feria at the intersection of Winston Churchill avenue and the Malecon is the Plaza de la Libertad. Although the plaza was built by Trujillo as part of the 1955 fair, it contains the Centro de los Heroes which commemorates forty martyrs in the struggle against Trujillo. The plaza is flanked by two parallel rows of 2.5 meter (8 feet) tall panels showing the name and profile of each martyr. In the center of the plaza is a statue of a welcoming woman and a world globe with wings.

Paseo de los Indios (Mirador del Sur Park)

This 7 km. (4 mile) long park runs parallel to the Malecon between Winston Churchill and Luperon Avenues. The park was built by President Balaguer who frequently walks through the park in the afternoon with his bodyguards, despite the fact that he is 85-years-old. Trees and shrubs from every part of the country have been planted here. The park encompasses a man-made lake where visitors can rent boats, as well as bicycling trails, roller skating paths, jogging trails, and various sculptures including the Fountain of Poetry by the noted Spanish sculptor Juan de Avalo. The western part of the park contains subtropical vegetation including tall cacti and huge aloes. Most incredible are two natural caves along the southern edge of the park which have been transformed into an excellent underground restaurant, Meson de la Cava, and a very popular and classy disco, Guacara Taina. This disco is the largest on the island and can accommodate 2,000 dancers (and occasional bats) 33 meters (110 feet) underground. Both can be reached by driving along Avenida Mirador del Sur.

Plaza Criolla

Plaza Criolla is an uncrowded tourist shopping center on Avenida 27 de Febrero just west of Avenida Maximo Gomez and the Gran Hotel Lina. Several well run shops sell jewelry, paintings, artisan goods, and foodstuffs to foreign tourists and affluent Dominicans. There is a good French restaurant, La Fromagerie, as well as an enjoyable tavern, La Ceniza. Prices are generally not as low as in Mercado Modelo but Plaza Criolla is clean, much less crowded and very convenient with ample parking.

Faro a Colon (Columbus Lighthouse)

The Faro a Colon is a huge structure constructed by the Balaguer administration in the southeast part of Santo Domingo, east of the Ozama River. The massive structure in the form of a horizontal cross is faintly reminiscent of an Egyptian pyramid and houses the remains of Christopher Columbus, as well as seven floors of exhibits related to the role of Spanish culture in the Americas. The Faro a Colon is solidly constructed (reinforced concrete) with a horizontal (rather than vertical) orientation to withstand future hurricanes or earthquakes and to serve as a cultural bridge into the next century.

The Faro a Colon concept has been around in one form or another since the mid-19th century and the actual structure was designed in 1929 by Joseph L. Gleave, an English architect. Gleave won an international competition by using a cross motif which the Dominicans believe corresponds well with Columbus' original beliefs. According to Dominican historians, Columbus called upon the inhabitants of Santo Domingo to:

Raise crosses everywhere to praise God. This land belongs to Christians. This is a message to be preserved forever.

The monument is designed as a lighthouse memorial with 135 reflectors on the roof which will project a cross into the sky. Under ideal conditions the light will be seen for hundreds of miles in the Caribbean. The lighthouse will have its own energy source and its light is said to be roughly as strong as 195 million light bulbs. The project cost at least US$70 million, a not insignificant sum for a country with a per capita income of less than US$1,000. Construction started in 1986 and was completed in time for the 500th year celebrations in 1992. President Balaguer steadfastly proceeded with the Faro project despite widespread criticism from those who felt these financial resources could be better used elsewhere.

To reach the Faro a Colon from downtown Santo Domingo, take 27 de Febrero west until it crosses the Ozama river on the Duarte bridge. Take the first right (just before a pedestrian causeway over the road) and continue straight for 1 km. (.7 miles). Turn left at the sign for Mirador del Este and continue straight for 1 km. (.7 miles) until the Faro appears straight ahead.

Parking is to the left (north) of the monument. From the parking area turn right and proceed 2.4 km. (1.5 miles) if you want to see Los Tres Ojos on the other end of the Parque del Este. The park is an enjoyable area to stroll and an amusement train carries people around the park.

National Aquarium

The National Aquarium is an extremely impressive facility located not far from Faro a Colon on Avenida Espana along the south coast on the eastern side of the Ozama River. Most travelers would expect to find such a sophisticated aquarium only in relatively rich countries in Europe or the United States. The aquarium contains an impressive collection of marine life including electric eels, piranhas, barracudas, sharks and giant turtles. The building is attractive and at one point visitors can walk under and around a huge transparent tank filled with fish. The aquarium is surrounded by a large park along the ocean on the east side, and the Ozama River and Espana Avenue (see map and follow directions for the Faro a Colon). The Aquarium has a snack bar and is open daily 10am–6pm. Admission is RD$5 for adults, RD$2 for students.

Parque de Los Tres Ojos (Three Eyes Park)

This park is located 5 km. (3 miles) east of Duarte Bridge over the Ozama River on Avenida las Americas (on the route to the airport). Tres Ojos Park is on the opposite (eastern) end of the Mirador del Este Park from the Faro a Colon and a visit can easily be combined with a trip to the Faro. Watch for a sign on the right side; parking is available near the cave entrance. After paying RD$4 visitors descend on a steep stairway down to a network of paths around the lakes.

The park is essentially a huge natural cave containing three freshwater underground lakes (the eyes) fed by an underground river. The third and largest underground lake is surrounded by

lush vegetation and all the caves are filled with interesting stalag-
mites and stalactites. A fourth lake fills the crater of an inactive
volcano and can only be reached by a small boat operated by
local people using hand pulleys (an additional RD$2). Sunlight
filters in from above for most of the walk so flashlights are not
necessary. The spacious Los Tres Ojos caves should be seen.
Arrive early in the day to beat the rush. The park is open every
day from 8am to 5pm.

La Caleta Submarine National Park

This unique underwater park was established in 1987 and is
located 23 km. (14 miles) east of Santo Domingo where the
road to the airport forks to the right along the shore. La Caleta
encompasses a large ornamental pool as well as many almond
trees and an underwater reef. The park contains half a dozen
ancient Taino graves in a thatched roof museum. There is a
small sandy beach area from which scuba divers embark in small
motor boats for the short trip out to the reef. The maximum
depth of the underwater portion of the park is 180 meters (590
feet) and its principal attraction is the submerged ship *Hickory*.
The *Hickory* was deliberately sunk in 1984 to create an artificial
reef which would protect marine life and encourage it to prolifer-
ate. In most places the depth varies between 10 to 50 meters
(33–164 feet) depending on the growth of coral reefs; colorful
fish are attracted to the area as a prime feeding ground. Scuba
divers are welcome and the reefs are a great place to view marine
life.

Engombe

On the western outskirts of Santo Domingo stand the ruins of a
16th century Moorish-gothic manor house and sugar plantation
called Engombe. Although some restoration work was done in
1963 to prevent further deterioration, the main building has no

roof and most of the second floor is missing. However, the double arcade and the walls and window sills remain standing. The old mansion is flanked by the plantation's chapel with its roof and altar intact. Ruins of a smaller building, either a stable or the slaves quarters, can be found nearby. The Haina River is just down the road and could easily be seen from the house if the area were not overgrown with foliage. This quiet spot gives the visitor a sense of what life was like on the old plantations. According to official records, the property was formerly called Santa Ana de Engombe and was sold in 1762 by Francisco Pepin Gonzalez, an official of the Real Audiencia to Lorenco Angulo, another leading Spanish official. Hundreds of slaves were growing and cutting sugar cane on this land in its heyday, all for the benefit of a Spanish family living like royalty in this very house.

The ruins are on part of a large farm that was confiscated from Trujillo's brother, Hector Bienvenido Trujillo, in 1962 and given by the government to the Autonomous University of Santo Domingo (UASD). To visit Engombe (which is now also the name of the neighborhood), head west on 27 de Febrero until reaching Avenida Luperon and Plaza Independencia, which is easily recognizable by the tall arch and huge flag. In the center of Plaza Independencia is a famous sculpture by Juan de Avalo in which the Unknown Soldier is portrayed as a dying man in the arms of his mother (the nation). Turn right off the traffic circle just past the government building labeled "INESPRE." Proceed to the next roundabout and turn right at the third road, between Codetel on the right and Industria de Pintura on the left. Continue 320 meters (.2 miles) to where the paved road ends and comes to a T. Bear right at the green building labeled Colmado Mabel and continue straight down this very rough dirt road bordered by houses for 2 km. (1.3 miles) until you see a gate on the left with the sign for the UASD. The Engombe ruins are on the grounds of an agricultural research station and the university personnel are generally cooperative when a visitor arrives at the gate asking to see the ruins. Proceed straight ahead past the chicken pens and dairy farm down the dirt track. Just

1.6 km. (1 mile) from the gate turn right and continue 320 meters (.2 miles) until you reach the ruins. At the time of writing, this area had not been developed for tourists and there were no signs.

Palave

The 17th-century Palave house is situated among sugar cane fields in pleasant countryside just west of Santo Domingo. The old manor house is on top of a small hill apart from the nearby town which bears its name. The building has been partially restored but there are no signs or guides at the site. Visitors can wander from room to room and look out over the beautiful local scenery. The house has the same style of bench windows found in the Alcazar and was built with thick walls to withstand attack from outside. The main entrance has four columns and the original two story house was large enough for perhaps as many as thirty people. The roof and the second floor are missing but the main walls are completely intact.

Visiting Palave is worth the effort to see a 17th century manor house surrounded by sugar cane fields much as it was three hundred years ago. To reach Palave follow the directions to Plaza Independencia (see Engombe above) and then continue on 27 de Febrero Avenue for about 14 km. (9 miles) and take a left on the road to Manoguayabo. Continue straight on this road for 1.6 km. (1 mile) until passing the National Police Operations Center on the right. Continue straight, crossing a small stone bridge, and turn right after another 1 km. (.6 miles) on a dirt road among the sugar cane fields where there are signs for Canetilla Aramilla and Repuestos Julisa. Palave is down this road 3 km. (1.8 miles) on the left shortly after passing a small cemetery. An old sign partially obscured by a tree says "Casa Palave." The house is just barely visible in the distance and can be reached by driving carefully along a dirt track. At the time of writing there was no admission charge.

CHAPTER 9

Southeast

Heading east from Santo Domingo along the south coast the traveler can find well developed tourist facilities. To get out of Santo Domingo going east, take Avenida 27 de Febrero and cross the Ozama River on the Duarte Bridge. Follow signs for Las Americas International Airport (29 km., 18 miles to the west). At the airport turnoff follow signs for Boca Chica. The highway is a pleasant drive along the ocean. Beware of policemen with white pith helmets manning informal speed traps who like nothing better than supplementing their meager incomes with bribes from speeding tourists.

Boca Chica

Boca Chica is situated 42 km. (26 miles) from the capital and serves as a popular local getaway on weekends. The exclusive Club Nautico de Santo Domingo is a private yacht club in Boca Chica not usually open to the public. Boca Chica is a reef protected ocean lagoon with a sandy beach. Generally free of rocks and not more than 1.5 meters (5 feet) deep, the beach is ideal for children. Two small islands lie in the lagoon, Isla de Pinos (named after its pine trees) and the small, mangrove covered Isla de Matica. Given its proximity to Santo Domingo, Boca Chica gets crowded and noisy (mopeds and jetskis) on weekends. Surf-boards, catamarans and windsurfing gear can be rented at the beach. The beach is built up with small hotel/restaurants and is reportedly a good place to meet local people. Plenty of tourist hotels (see Appendix) and restaurants are available in Boca Chica.

Juan Dolio

The next resort area to the east is Juan Dolio, just 20 km. (12 miles) further along the coastal road. Juan Dolio is home to a number of high quality hotels easily reached from the main highway (see Appendix). One good place to stay right on the beach is Metro Hotel. This hotel has a reef just offshore which provides visitors with an excellent (and convenient) place for snorkeling. A bit further along the main road on the right is GO Kart Bahn where go karts can be rented. A number of good restaurants are nearby, including El Sueno (Italian).

San Pedro de Macoris

Further to the east (64 km., 40 miles from Santo Domingo) is the town of San Pedro de Macoris, the fifth largest town in the country. The name *Macoris* refers to the Indian tribe which once inhabited this area. The modern history of San Pedro began in 1822 when Dominican families fleeing Haitian incursions to the west settled in the area. A modern port facility was completed in 1867 and the town grew rapidly as a center of the sugar industry. From the bridge over the Higuamo River, the Church of St. Peter the Apostle can be seen to the right in the distance. Follow signs for the port (*puerto*) and turn to the right. Continue straight through town until you reach the fairly modern church built in 1913. For those travelers without cars, the bus station is directly across from the church. From the church continue on the main road along the waterfront until you come to the Malecon where there are a number of restaurants (Portofino is inexpensive and good). Probably the best hotel in town is the Macorix on the waterfront; it's easy to find. Other inexpensive local hotels are available (see Appendix).

San Pedro is home to the Universidad Central del Este (Central University of the East) with thousands of students from around the country. Baseball is very popular with a season from October through January and taking in a game at the Tetelo Vargas Stadium is recommended. The town is noteworthy for having supplied more major league baseball players to the United States than any other Dominican town. To reach the stadium from the main road from the west, continue straight through the first roundabout (not toward the port), and the stadium is on the left next to the road for Hato Mayor. There is a community of people in town called *cocolos*, descended from English-speaking sugar cane cutters brought in from other Caribbean islands who maintain a distinct cultural identity. Some of the cocolo customs, such as the parade of the Guloyes on June 29 (the day of the city's patron saint) and the *Dance Salvaje* (wild dance) are still practiced. San Pedro de Macoris will be the Dominican terminus of the ferry from Puerto Rico, expected to resume operations in 1992 or 1993.

Los Haitises National Park

To the east in a remote part of the country south of Samana bay is the Los Haitises National Park, a 1,200-square km. (463 square miles) wilderness area which is particularly noteworthy from a geological point of view. The park was created in 1976. Access by land is almost impossible as there are no roads in the park and most travelers arrive in boats from Samana or from the nearby town of Sabana de la Mar.

To reach Sabana de la Mar from Santo Domingo, proceed to San Pedro de Macoris (see above) and head due north. As you enter San Pedro de Macoris from the west, continue past the first roundabout and then turn left just before the Estadio Tetelo Varga on your left. Continue straight through town and into flat sugar cane country for another 35 km. (22 miles) until you reach Hato Mayor. The road is paved and traffic will be fairly light. Once in Hato Mayor take the northern route, not the road east to El Seibo, and continue for another 42 km. (26 miles) along a recently paved road. The terrain becomes more rugged and the road winds around quite a bit but is in good shape.

Entering Sabana de la Mar the road passes a military zone on the left and a bit further along is a yellow building with a sign for the Direccion Nacional de Parques, Parque Nacional los Haitises on the left. Information about the park and a map is available for viewing. At the time of writing, the administrator of the park was a young man named Miguel Mateo (tel. 556-7333) who can arrange boat tours if he is contacted long enough in advance. The park service likes to provide transportation, or at least be kept informed, when travelers enter the park. If the park service is unable to provide transportation, an alternative is to find a local fisherman to take you over. Follow signs for the *muelle* (pier) as you drive into town and it won't be difficult to find local fishermen.

Near the pier is the quiet town square, with plenty of benches and shade trees as well as a refreshing sea breeze all day. Across the street is a pleasant, if somewhat basic, outdoors restaurant where you can order pizza, chicken, beer, etc., at reasonable prices. Across the street is a popular disco. The largest hotel is Villa Suiza (see Appendix) and there are a couple of other rustic options.

Those travelers attempting to reach the park with the help of a local fisherman must be sure to negotiate a price in advance for the trip. At the time of writing, it cost RD$500–1000 to hire a boat (not per person) to, around and back from the park, which generally takes most of the day. Travelers should take their own food and water, as well as protection from the sun and a flashlight. It takes about 1½ to 2 hours to reach the most interesting areas. The boats pass beautiful, untouched shoreline as well as hundreds of pelicans diving in groups to fish the coastal waters. After about an hour the coast changes to karst, a large area of limestone formations characterized by sinks and ravines. The area was formed 25 to 40 million years ago by voluminous masses of coral rock which emerged through earth movements. The park is filled with small conical hills and the highest elevation is only 485 meters above sea level. Limestone caves are found in the park complete with Taino petroglyphs and bats. Three fascinating caves along the ocean are La Arena, La Linea and San Gabriel. The park service has done a good job of marking the caves, even to the point of putting a detailed map in the entrance to the Cueva de San Gabriel (the largest). Most of the caves can be explored without a flashlight because the limestone has many fissures allowing in sunlight. The predominate flora are broad-leafed plants, a wide variety of ferns, bromelias, orchids, lianas as well as trees such as silk-cotton, Indian cedar, Hispaniolan mahogany and mangrove. Most common birds are the brown pelican, American frigate bird, little blue heron, northern tacana, and occasionally the Hispaniolan parakeet. The boat trip to Parque Nacional de los Haitises is a thoroughly enjoyable experience, as long as you're not prone to seasickness.

From Sabana de la Mar it is possible to proceed east along the coast to Miches. The road is very poor and the trip takes a long time even though Miches is only 42 km. (26 miles) away. Miches is in a particularly remote part of the country with virtually no tourism. The town is noteworthy as the primary jumping off point for illegal immigrants trying to get through the Mona Straight to Puerto Rico. According to local people, boats leave Miches at least once a week and charge RD$4,000–5,000 per person. There is a dirt track south from Miches through the mountains which eventually reaches El Seibo. This route is very slow and remote, and is not recommended.

Just 17 km. (11 miles) east of Miches along the coast road are the Redonda and Limon lagoons, a government nature reserve. While access may be difficult for visitors, the mangrove covered reserve area provides sanctuary to several types of birds including pied-billed grebe, common gallinule, great egret, black-crowned night heron, roseate spoonbill and northern pintail.

La Romana

Located 38 km. (24 miles) east of San Pedro de Macoris is La Romana, an impressive modern town developed largely by U.S. companies (most recently Gulf & Western) to meet the needs of the sugar industry. As in San Pedro growth began in the mid-19th century with the construction of port facilities for the sugar cane industry. The Central Romana Sugar Mill was first built in 1917 and expanded four times to the point where it is now one of the largest in the world. The name La Romana comes from a Roman scale originally used to weigh sugar exports at the port. With roughly 90,000 inhabitants the town is the fourth largest in the Dominican Republic. La Romana is still a sugar town and there are signs of the industry everywhere. La Romana company employs roughly 18,000 people in the sugar industry. Trucks carry cane cutters to and from work during the harvest season and a sweetish, molasses-like odor often fills the air.

Driving into town from the west, Cabanas Tio Tom (Uncle Tom's Cabins, see Appendix) is on the right side shortly before the right turnoff for Higuey. Continuing straight on the main road into La Romana the modern Micheli baseball stadium is on the left and an old railroad steam engine on the right. A bit further on the right is a large outdoor vegetable market. On the left are Hotel Bolivar and Hotel Frano, as well as a Honda rent-a-car. Near the central park, Parque Duarte, are a number of reasonable restaurants, including Don Quijote's. An excellent Italian restaurant is La Casita (556-5509) on the eastern edge of town just west of the Dulce river (on C. Docoudray 57). Around the corner down the street is the Libra Apart-hotel (556-3787, 11 C. Gil).

On the other side of the Dulce River is the Casa de Campo complex covering 7,000 acres. Casa de Campo has a nice sandy beach (Las Minitas which is man-made and can be visited by tourists), 750 luxurious rooms, yachting facilities, 13 clay tennis courts (10 lighted), 19 swimming pools, two 18-hole golf courses (one along the ocean), hundreds of horses and polo grounds. Visitors can learn to play polo from October through May. Trail riding and skeet shooting are also possible, as are innumerable aquatic sports. There are also a host of privately owned villas on the grounds visited by such luminaries as Oscar de la Renta and Henry Kissinger, as well as most top officials of the Dominican government. To reach Casa de Campo, proceed toward La Romana, turn right just past the Shell station on the left at the traffic light with a the sign for Higuey. Cross the La Romana sugar company's train tracks, continue straight through town past the sign for Central Romana sugar company on the right over the bridge on the Dulce River and then through a traffic circle. On the right is a turnoff for the Punta Aguila International Airport where flights come in from Santo Domingo, as well as the American Eagle flights from Puerto Rico. For Casa de Campo continue straight ahead, for Dominicus Beach and Higuey, turn left at the next intersection.

One very pleasant spot near La Romana (take the marked road northeast from Casa de Campo) is Altos de Chavon, a picturesque village built in 16th century Italian style on a hilltop. The village was built by local craftsmen in 1978 under the direction of Italian architect Roberto Copa. In the center of the village is the Church of St. Stanislaus, named after the patron saint of Poland in honor of Pope John Paul II who visited in 1979. There are five good restaurants: El Sombrero (Mexican 7–11pm), La Pizzella (Italian 7–11pm), La Fonda, Cafeteria La Casa and Casa del Rio (French 7–11pm) overlooking the beautiful Chavon river valley. The view of the Chavon river winding slowly toward mountains in the distance through the unspoiled countryside is fantastic and on a clear day you can see for miles. An impressive 5,000-seat

Roman amphitheater for concerts, numerous art galleries, boutiques, and art workshops are melded together in Altos de Chavon in the natural coral setting. A charming little museum of Taino Indian artifacts makes for an interesting visit. A local design school affiliated with the Parson School of Design brings in a number of international students. Genesis, the local disco, opens at 10pm. Every February an artisan fair takes place in Altos de Chavon when artists from all over the country get together. The only hotel in Altos de Chavon is La Posada and reservations are handled by Casa de Campo.

Bayahibe

The unspoiled town of Bayahibe is a peaceful little seaside village 15 km. (9 miles) east of La Romana. Boats can be rented for less than RD$1,500 per day to go to Saona Island (part of the National Park of the East). Small streams run into the ocean, making it possible to swim along the beach in either salt or fresh water. Local hotels include Hotel Bayahibe (10 rooms and a generator, RD$200–RD$300) and Hotel Tranquera (rents horses and cabanas). Picturesque restaurants include Tamarinde, La Tranquera, Adrian, Bayahibe (RD$50–100) and Bahia.

Not far from Bayahibe is the Dominicus Beach Village Resort (58 basic rooms, rustic decor) situated on 1,200 hectares (3,000 acres) of vast and solitary beach. Most visitors and many staff at Dominicus are young Italians who contribute to its charm and good food. To find Dominicus take the left from La Romana at the intersection just past Punta Aguila airport and proceed for 8 km. (5 miles) until the road descends into a dramatic cut through the coral rock and you cross the Chavon River. After 5 km. (3 miles) there is an intersection where the left fork takes you to Higuey and the right to Bayahibe and Puerto Laguna (also known as Dominicus Beach). After about 8 km. (5 miles) you will see Restaurante Amozonia (Italian) on the left in the middle of nowhere. Continue 10 km. (6 miles) and you will eventually see a sign for Bayahibe down a dirt road on your right. Continue straight for Dominicus Beach or right for Bayahibe.

Higuey

The town of Higuey, with roughly 93,000 inhabitants, lies 32 km. (20 miles) northeast of the turnoff for Dominicus. Higuey is the home of the Basilica de Nuestra Senora de la Altagracia, a huge stone structure built in 1952 by a French architect in a unique style which does not resemble anything else in the country. The sect devoted to the Virgin of Altagracia originated here and the monumental basilica houses her miraculous shrine. Each January 24 a huge pilgrimage marches to the basilica to honor the Virgin, as well as to seek good health and spiritual well-being. Worship of the Virgin of Altagracia goes back to early colonial times; the first procession occurred in 1669 following a promise made by Spanish colonists fighting the French.

After entering town from the south, take the left fork which becomes Avenida Hermanos Trejo. Continue straight to find the basilica; it towers over the town and is not hard to reach. Higuey has a good restaurant called El Gran Gourmet to the right just off Avenida Hermanos Trejo on General Santana. Look for the three large crosses on the right about two blocks before coming to the basilica. Another interesting stop is the original 16th century church (rebuilt in 1881 following an earthquake) which can be found by driving past the Gran Gourmet on C. General Santana. The old church contains an original 16th century anonymous painting of the Virgin of Altagracia framed in gold which was a present from Pope Pius X. A silver throne is used to carry the painting and a golden crown through the streets of Higuey during religious processions. A number of inexpensive local hotels are available, especially on Calle Colon (see Appendix).

The Punta Cana Luxury Hotels

To continue on to the Punta Cana peninsula pass the entrance to the basilica on your left and continue down Hermanos Trejo

until the street ends and you are facing a large sign indicating
Bavaro Beach to the right. Turn right here and continue on out
of the town on the paved road. The area to the east of Higuey
is quite sparsely populated so travelers with vehicles should make
sure they have adequate gasoline. Proceed 7 km. (4 miles) to the
town of Otra Banda and turn right at the police station. (This
turnoff was unmarked at the time of writing and travelers should
be careful not to miss it.)

   After heading east for 27 km. (17 miles) along this paved road
there is a turnoff for Bavaro Beach on the left. Continue straight
for Club Med (11 km., 7 miles) and Punta Cana Beach Resort
(16 km., 10 miles). The privately owned and operated Punta
Cana Airport is 8 km. (5 miles) further on the left side of the
main road. Certain charter flights filled with tourists land here
to save time and avoid congestion at the country's larger airports.

Bavaro Beach Resort

   Bavaro Beach Resort is a large and well run tourist complex
located another 12 km. (7 miles) to the north of the turnoff. The
hotel has enough space to house 3,000 guests at one time. There
are four large hotel buildings: Hotel Beach (600 double rooms),
Hotel Garden (400 double rooms), Aparthotel Golf (126 apartments) and Hotel Casino (64 suites, 104 double rooms). The
complex boasts 15 bars, 9 restaurants (4 buffet, 2 grills and 3 a
la carte), 3 discos, 8 tennis courts, 7 swimming pools (including
3 for children), a golf course and a large casino with the capacity
to hold 400 people.

   Guests at Bavaro Beach are under various inclusive plans
which generally cover meals and sports activities such as windsurfing, water skiing, etc., along the excellent beach. The vast
majority of guests tend to be northern Europeans on group tours
who spend their entire holiday at the resort rather than visiting
the rest of the country. There is no reason for independent travel-

ers not to stay at Bavaro but reservations are advisable (see Appendix).

Club Med

Club Med is a smaller scale operation than Bavaro Beach with 380 rooms located along the beach on a 70 acre property. As is the case worldwide, the Dominican Club Med provides nightly entertainment for its guests as well as a host of activities during the day.

Punta Cana Beach Resort

Punta Cana Beach Resort is located just 7 km. (4 miles) east of the Punta Cana Airport on a 105 acre property. The resort has 340 double rooms in townhouses and separate villas. The ambiance is very relaxing and visitors can stroll along the empty beach for miles. Horseback riding and water sports are options during the day; the resort provides nightly entertainment.

Estate of Juan Ponce de Leon

The Casa de Ponce de Leon provides a sense of how rural life in Hispaniola was during the 16th century. The house is situated in a rural area away from any other man-made structure and was restored by the Dominican and Puerto Rican governments. Juan Ponce de Leon built the house in 1505–06 prior to his conquest of Puerto Rico in 1508 and his subsequent adventures in Florida. The house contains original furniture, armor and various artifacts and is built solidly enough to withstand a siege. The entrance fee in RD$10 and a knowledgeable guide can explain everything you want to hear if you understand Spanish. The grounds surrounding the house include a pleasant picnic area and lots of open space.

To find the Estate of Juan Ponce de Leon follow the directions (above) to Higuey from la Romana but turn right at the second roundabout 16 km. (10 miles) after the turnoff for Bayahibe. Proceed 7 km. (4 miles) south to San Rafael de Yuma and take the left fork toward the center of town (the right fork leads to Boca de Yuma and the National Park of the East). On the left about 1 km. (.6 miles) after the fork is a (unmarked) dirt road which leads to the Ponce de Leon Estate.

Boca de Yuma

Boca de Yuma, another 10 km. (6 miles) down the road (taking the right fork as you arrive in San Rafael de Yuma), is a small fishing village on the mouth of the Yuma River. This unpretentious little town is frequently the scene for international fishing contests, as well as being a popular stop yet not touched by tourism for international yachts. However, the town is not yet frequented by tourists so that hotels and restaurants are fairly basic. To find the National Park of the East after arriving in town, turn right on the dirt road at the Marina de Guardia (navy) office just one block in from the ocean. Continue along this dirt road out of town passing Hotel Vias del Este (inexpensive) on the right. National Parks in the Dominican Republic are very different from in the United States, so don't be surprised that the road seems to lead nowhere. Drive slowly on this fairly rough road for 1.6 km. (1 mile) until a cemetery is on the left with an unmarked turnoff to the right. The right turn leads about 200 meters (1/10 of a mile) to the unmarked but accessible Berna Cave (flashlight and equipment are needed and a guide advisable), which is roughly 180 meters (200 yards) deep. Instead of turning right at the cemetery, continue straight to reach the National Park of the East.

National Park of the East

Another important attraction in the area is the relatively unknown National Park of the East, a 430 square km. (166 square miles) expanse of wilderness along the ocean with no paved roads and few visitors. The park stretches more than 25 km. (16 miles) from Dominicus Beach resort in the west to Boca del Yuma in the east and includes the 110 square km. (42 square mile) Sanoa Island. Dominican rangers are willing to conduct visitors (who are few and far between) to various sights such as caves within the park. Maps are difficult to obtain. To reach the park from Dominicus simply walk west along the beach for a couple of miles to a fence and a sign indicating the park boundary. Not far from the unlocked fence is a modest house with a resident park ranger who knows the park well. Bring a flashlight to explore the caves; he won't have one.

To reach the eastern (least traveled) edge of the park, take the left fork toward Higuey at the intersection (see above) where Bayahibe is to the right. Drive 16 km. (10 miles) and turn right (instead of left to Higuey) at the intersection with a sign for San Rafael de Yuma. Proceed another 7 km. (4.6 miles) until you reach the town of San Rafael de Yuma. Take the right fork to continue directly to Boca de Yuma and the National Park of the East. Continue straight from the turnoff another 2.7 km. (1.7 miles) to the park entrance (see above). At the time of writing, one sign marked the gate, but it was hanging on its side. As you near the gate, a Dominican government ranger will approach you suspiciously (tourists are rare here) from the house to the right of the gate and will probably carry some sort of primitive rifle. Have no fear, he means well. Tourists are free to explore the park and can leave vehicles near the gate within sight of the ranger's house. Dominican rangers don't speak English and will appear very informal, but they will generally try to be helpful (especially for a tip).

Two main trails cross through the park, one along the coast and the other through the interior toward Bayahibe, more than 32 km. (20 miles) away. The coastal trail affords spectacular scenery and reaches the ocean soon after leaving the gate. As in certain U.S. national parks, privately owned cattle may be seen grazing in the park. Both trails are mainly over hard coral rock and are rugged in places. They are not formally marked, but are not difficult to discern. Travelers are strongly advised to bring plenty of water and hats if they attempt to go for any appreciable distance along these trails. Note: To complete the circuit would require hiking a distance of rougly 96 km. (60 miles) and is recommended only for experienced hikers equipped to camp along the way.

The National Park of the East is an extremely important sanctuary for birds and animals, some of which are endangered species. The solendon is an ancient insect-eating mammal native to the island; it has a small body (30 cm., 12 inches) and a long snout. Another native animal is the hutia, a furry rodent and skillful climber. Both the solendon and the hutia are nocturnal animals which live in caves or dry tree trunks and are in danger of extinction. Other endangered species found in the park are bottlenose dolphin, West Indian manatee and the white-crowned pigeon. Among the most common birds in the park are the Hispaniolan parrot, red-footed booby, barn owl, stygian owl, plain pigeon, herring gull, American frigate bird and brown pelican. A number of caves can be found within the park, especially in the eastern part. The western part of the park near Bayahibe and Isla Saona are the most visited areas, and some poor local people live permanently within the park's boundaries.

SANTIAGO DE LOS CABALLEROS

LAS CARITAS, LAGO ENRIQUILLO

MONUMENTO DE LA RESTAURACION, SANTIAGO

SANTIAGO DE LOS CABALLEROS

La Mansion, San Jose de las Matas

Countryside near Pico Duarte

Undeveloped coast near Samana

Local business, Las Terrenas, Samana Peninsula

Karst formations, Los Haitises National Park

TYPICAL ROCKY SHORE
ALONG EAST COAST

BREACHING HUMPBACK WHALE, SAMANA BAY

ALCAZAR, SANTO DOMINGO

LA ATARANZA,
SANTO DOMINGO

FEMALE OBELISK, EL MALECON, SANTO DOMINGO

Plaza de los Heroes, Santo Domingo

Torre de Homenaje, Santo Domingo

Typical street, Santo Domingo

Jaragua Hotel, Santo Domingo

EL MALECON, SANTO DOMINGO

LOWER LEFT: MUSEO CASAS REALES, SANTO DOMINGO
LOWER RIGHT: CASA DE GARGOYLES, SANTO DOMINGO

Calle de las Damas, Santo Domingo

Panteon Nacional, Santo Domingo

City wall and Alcazar, Santo Domingo

Casa de Cordon,
Santo Domingo

PLAZA DE LOS HEROES, SANTO DOMINGO

CATHEDRAL BASILICA MENOR SANTA MARIA, SANTO DOMINGO

UPPER LEFT: CATHEDRAL BASILICA MENOR SANTA MARIA, SIDE VIEW
UPPER RIGHT: TAINO PETROGLYPH, LOS HAITISES NATIONAL PARK

CAVE INHABITED BY ANCIENT TAINO, LOS HAITISES NATIONAL PARK

TOP: La Isabela, first European settlement north coast
ABOVE: Cibao Valley
BELOW: Convento de Regina Angelorum, Santo Domingo

ABOVE: Convento de los
Dominicanos, Santo Domingo

RIGHT: Columbus statue, Plaza
de Colon

BELOW: Porcelain Museum,
Santo Domingo

EL CONDE,
SANTO DOMINGO

HAITIAN PAINTINGS FOR SALE ALONG EL CONDE, SANTO DOMINGO

CHAPTER 10

Dominican Mountains

The Dominican Republic contains a unique mountainous region (cordillera central) seldom visited by foreign tourists. There are two mountains in excess of 3,050 meters (10,000 ft) above sea level, by far the highest in the Caribbean. The two mountains are Pico Duarte (3,175 m., 10,417 ft.) and La Pelona (3,138 m., 10,294 ft). Two national parks straddling the high peak region are J. Armando Bermudez and J. Del Carmen Ramirez. The nearby delightful mountain towns of Constanza and Jarabacoa should be visited.

Constanza

The town of Constanza has 43,000 inhabitants and is located 1,097 meters (3,600 ft) above sea level, considerably higher than any other sizeable town in the Dominican Republic. Constanza is situated in a high valley of the cordillera central surrounded by 1,800 m. (5,900 ft.) high mountains with pine trees. The climate is dramatically different from Santo Domingo and provides an escape from the heat and humidity during the summer. The town has a large ethnic Japanese population which has contributed much to the impressive development of a diversified agricultural base, including strawberries, lettuce, apples and a variety of other temperate climate fruits and vegetables. Constanza is also the center of a large flower growing (and exporting) industry.

To reach Constanza take the Autopista Duarte north (reached by heading west of Avenida John F. Kennedy). Roughly 16 km. (10 miles) out of Santo Domingo is a toll booth (RD$.50). From there continue on the main highway for 66 km. (41 miles) until reaching a left turn for Constanza, marked by a green and blue sign on the right side of the road as well as a red Bermudez sign. The road up the mountain is well built, quite steep and affords an excellent view of the Cibao valley. The road passes through forests of pine trees, commercial flower farms and coffee plantations. After 31 km. (19 miles) the road comes to the town of El Rio where a turnoff on a rough dirt road to the right leads to Jarabacoa. The road to Constanza is 49 km. (30 miles) long after leaving Autopista Duarte and runs sharply uphill amid fantastic scenery.

The largest hotel in town and the one with the most impressive surroundings is the Swiss Chalet. Sadly the chalet has been particularly badly managed by the government to the point where it can hardly be called a hotel. The physical plant is impressive—large halls, balustrade, and terraces, a dining room with picture windows all overlooking beautiful mountain scenery. However, at the time of writing no food or drink was available (save Dominican coffee in the morning), a major effort was necessary to obtain such basic items as towels and toilet paper (forget soap or running water in the wash basin), room keys were unavailable, much of the downstairs was flooded, the rooms were filthy with paint literally falling off the walls, and the staff played loud music all night. Needless to say the rooms are not screened to keep out mosquitoes. All in all, if visitors bring camping gear and manage to keep the staff reasonably quiet, the place is bearable—the view counts for a lot.

The Swiss Chalet is located on the southern edge of town on the road to San Jose de Ocoa. Entering Constanza from the east turn left just before the Texaco station. The hotel can be seen from town, a large white structure to the right of the road. Proceed down this road for 1.6 km. (1 mile) and take the (unmarked) paved road to the right where a sign for a strawberry field says "Fresadom 300 mts." The Japanese club (members only) is 160 m. (.1 miles) further down the road on the left. The hotel is on the edge of a wooded area near a number of hiking trails that the visitor can take to explore the surrounding countryside. Many impressive local farms have intricate irrigation systems and well constructed houses which belong to local Japanese families. As an influential minority, the Japanese community appears to take a low profile and no Japanese restaurants or hotels are found in the area.

One alternative to staying in the Swiss Chalet is Mi Cabana near the center of town on Calle Rufino Espinosa. The rooms are clean (air-conditioning is not needed at this altitude) and a reasonably good restaurant is nearby. Other local hotels are: Margarita, Brisas del Valle and Sobeyda. A reasonable restaurant popular with locals is Lorenzo's near the center of town.

Departing Constanza is easiest along the main (paved) road but there is an alternate route via San Jose de Ocoa to the south. This road is very bad—completely unpaved until you reach San Jose, although the mountain scenery is spectacular. The road goes through the Valle Nuevo Nature Reserve, a large 409 km. (158 square miles) high plateau which is mainly covered with creolean pine and Dominican magnolia trees. A huge forest fire did quite a bit of damage in 1983 but the forest is recuperating. Prominent birds along this route incude: rufous-collared sparrow, Antillean siskin, stripe-headed tanager, pine warbler, white-winged warbler, blue-hooded euphonia and golden swallow. This trip should not be attempted without a high clearance four-wheel-drive vehicle and the traveler should allow at least three hours (no services along the way) to reach San Jose.

Jarabacoa

The other major mountain town, Jarabacoa (48,000 inhabitants), is more tourist oriented although most tourists are Dominicans.

Impressive vacation homes belonging to affluent Dominicans can be seen on certain streets. Numerous bars and restaurants, including several pizzerias, offer food to visitors. Three designated swimming spots can be found in nearby mountain rivers and horses can be rented for RD$40 per hour.

To reach Jarabacoa, either come across from the Constanza road to El Rio over 18 km. (11 miles) of rough and winding road (four-wheel-drive recommended) or drive directly over from the Autopista Duarte at La Vega. The turnoff for Jarabacoa is directly across from a Texaco station on the northern edge of La Vega, just past the La Vega Zona Franca on the left (marked by a red Bermudez sign). The turnoff is 109 km. (68 miles) north of the toll booth leaving Santo Domingo. Hotel de la Montaña is 11 km. (7 miles) after turning left off Autopista Duarte on the way to Jarabacoa. Hotel de la Montaña is a large and comfortable Dominican hotel with an excellent view of the mountains, a billiard table, a competent staff, good dining room and a large pool. Just across the road is the La Ganja Restaurant/Guest House.

Continuing up the road to Jarabacoa another 6.5 km. (4 miles) is a turnoff for El Salto de Jimenoa, a waterfall and swimming area. Turn right on a marked paved road and continue 5.6 km. (3.5 miles), always staying on the main road. After 120 meters (.1 miles) you pass the National School of Forestry on the right. At the end of the road take the right fork and drive up to the military post by the hydroelectric plant. Leave your vehicle in front of the military checkpoint and cross the bridge on foot. Turn left and walk directly over to the power plant. From the back of the power plant climb carefully along a large pipe and down the rocks over to the river. Continue upstream for about 800 meters (.5 miles) over smooth purple and blue rocks until you reach the waterfall and the pool below. There is a good view of the falls and the large sandy pool is a great place to swim. There is no admittance fee and guides are not needed.

From the main road to Jarabacoa as you enter town there is a marked turnoff for La Confluencia park at the first right after you cross the second (small) red bridge. La Confluencia park is easily accessible; just take the first right on a paved, two lane road through a quiet, residential area and continue 3 km. (2 miles) to the end of the road. Drive right to the water's edge where the Yaque del Norte and the Jimenoa rivers come together. There are horses to rent, vendors selling drinks and Dominican snacks and probably Dominican tourists in swimming. Note: Swim carefully—beware of strong currents. Those travelers seeking greater solitude can hike nearby paths along the rivers.

One of the most pleasant places to stay in Jarabacoa is the Hotel Pinar Dorado on the edge of town along the Constanza road. To find the hotel stay on the main road as it weaves through town, passes a military zone on the left and finally comes to an end in front of the Shell station. Turn left on the road to Constanza and continue for a short distance (all paved) until you see the hotel on the left. Hotel Pinar Dorado has a good (but not cheap) dining room, a pleasant pool and is reasonably well managed. Foreign visitors are not rare, but most visitors are Dominican tourists escaping from the heat in the lowlands. Airconditioning is not necessary at this altitude, but is available in a few rooms. The rooms are clean, have screens on the windows, are well maintained and—while not luxurious—are comfortable. Horses are available in the parking lot (RD$40 per hour) and the hotel staff will gladly arrange for guides to the local attractions.

One popular destination not far from Hotel Pinar Dorado is El Salto de Bayaguate (a waterfall) where you can walk or hike from the hotel. The trail is 800 meters (.5 miles) farther down the Constanza road from the hotel and is marked by a red Bermudez sign (with a slightly different spelling—which often happens in this country). It is possible to make it over this trail with a high clearance four-wheel-drive vehicle, but most people prefer horses. The waterfall is another 2.4 km. (1.5 miles) from the point where the trail leaves the Constanza road. At the end of the track there is an abandoned concrete building. At this point the trail bears right and follows the concrete path to the falls. The falls are a secluded place to swim and picnic.

Pico Duarte and the High Peak National Parks

Pico Duarte and La Pelona are the tallest peaks in the Caribbean and provide a glimpse of a unique tropical/temperate flora. These mountains lie in a particularly remote part of the country and it almost seems as if the Dominicans have done their best to keep them hidden. There are three official entrances, i.e., trails with national park offices, to the high peak region: Mata Grande via San Jose de las Matas (see Chapter 6) to the north, La Cienega (also known as Boca del Rios—via Jarabacoa) to the east, and from the south via the Saboneta dam past the Corral de los Indios and San Juan de la Maguana (see Chapter 7). The admission charge is RD$50 for foreigners (RD$20 for Dominicans) and all visitors are required to take along a guide. Trails are not marked and having a guide makes lots of sense and should not be resisted. The park service has established a flat rate of RD$50 per day for guides and RD$50 per day for mules.

The closest and most accessible entrance to the park region is La Cienega via Jarabacoa. To reach the park take the main road in Jarabacoa to the end and turn right at the Shell station (where you would turn left for Hotel Pinar Dorado) on the road called El Carmen. There are no gas stations on this road after leaving Jarabacoa so it is wise to leave with a full tank. Proceed 4 blocks downhill across a small bridge and take a sharp left onto a dirt road, known as the road to Manabao. Travelers without cars be advised that this is the point in Jarabacoa to catch public transportation to the base of Pico Duarte. A daily (except Sunday) bus costing RD$40 passes by between 12 noon and 2 pm and goes all the way to the trail head at La Cienaga. The daily bus starts out from La Cienaga at 7am Monday through Saturday. Alternatively more frequent buses run to the town of Manabao.

Turning left after the bridge, the building on the right is labeled "Ramirez Commercial." Continue straight (west) on this rough road for another 21 km. (13 miles) until you reach the town of Manabao. At a small hostel called Patria Muñoz in Manabao, travelers can stay for the night. From Manabao to La Cienega take the (unmarked) right turn directly across from the local police station. The road becomes unbelievably bad for the next 10 km. (6 miles) and should definitely not be attempted without a high clearance four-wheel-drive vehicle. The scenery is unbeatable along this route, but the driver will have scant opportunity to appreciate it unless he stops the vehicle. The trip to La Cienega is only 30 km. (19 miles) from Jarabacoa but takes roughly two hours. After arriving in La Cienega leave the vehicle parked under the care of a local resident and walk ahead about 200 meters along a dirt path to the park's entrance.

The Armando Bermudez National Park (766 square km., 296 square miles) was created by 1956, followed two years later by the adjacent Jose del Carmen Rodriguez National Park (764 square km., 295 square miles) to the south. The Comparticion River (stream) is the boundary between the two parks. These two parks contain the four highest peaks in the Caribbean: Pico Duarte (3,175 m., 10,417 feet), La Pelona (3138 m., 10,294 feet), La Rusilla (3,038 m., 9,965 feet) and Pico Yaque (2,760 m., 9,053 feet). These igneous rock mountains formed roughly 60 million years ago. Temperatures range between 12°C and 21° C (53° F and 70° F), and can drop as low as minus 8 °C (17° F) at dawn in December and January. At least twelve of the country's most important rivers begin within these two parks, including the Yaque River which passes through Santiago. These rivers are critical for the country's agriculture in the San Juan and Cibao valleys, as well as hydroelectric power for much of the region.

The current admission fee is RD$50 per person and can be paid in advance in Santo Domingo or at the local national park office. To arrange a permit in Santo Domingo contact the Eco-turista office in the Eugenia Maria de Hostos Park on Vicini Burgos Street near the male obelisk along the Malecon (tel. 221-4104/06, fax 689-3703). For most of the year travelers can simply show up in La Cienaga and make all necessary arrangements.

Park rules require that all visitors take along a guide. The visitor is free to choose a guide from the available pool of certi-fied local guides, but the park officials will gladly assist. Local people are poor and obtaining a guide is generally not difficult. More likely the unsuspecting tourist will agree to pay too high a price before reaching the park office. Groups of more than five people are required to take along an additional guide; one guide for each five people. The hike will generally take three to four days and visitors are expected to provide food for themselves and the guides. Food can be purchased locally at the beginning of the trip and the guides will cook rice, beans, canned meat, etc., for your dinner.

Water is found in fresh mountain streams and does not present any problem although some hikers believe water purification tablets are advisable. Hikers are advised to bring along a canteen for each person plus an extra one for the use of the guide. The path is steep and the climb is strenuous. Hikers who are not in excellent physical condition should bring extra mules to ride at least part of the way. Virtually all hikers should hire at least one mule to carry their provisions.

The round trip distance to Pico Duarte and back from La Cienaga is only 46 km. (29 miles), but the hike is so demanding that it seems to many much farther. The three designated camp-ing areas are located at: Los Tablones, La Comparticion and Valle del Tetero. Stream water is available near each of the campsites for washing. Each campground consists of a large wooden building with separate rooms for hikers and guides, a kitchen building and outhouses. Near the Valle del Tetero camp-ground is a large rock inscribed with Taino petroglyphs.

One sensible way to approach the climb is to hike to Valle Tetero the first day, to La Comparticion the second day, to the peak and back to La Comparticion the third day and back down the fourth day. Faster ascents are possible, but tend to deteriorate into endurance contests. Note: It is possible to make the trip starting from one entrance of the park and leaving from another, but such a journey requires complex logistical work and plenty of time. The relevant distances from Cienaga and elevations are as follows:

	Distance		Elevation	
	km	miles	meters	feet
La Cienaga	0	0	1040	3411
Los Tablones	4	2.5	1170	3838
Loma La Cotorra	9	5.6	1720	5642
Valle del Tetero (near Pico del Yaque)	14	8.7	2660	8725
La Comparticion	20	12.4	2460	8069
Pico Duarte	23	14.3	3175	10294

After leaving Los Tablones the steep ascent up Pico Yaque, the first mountain along the way, begins. The climate becomes appreciably colder during the ascent and warm clothing (sweaters, hats) and warm sleeping bags are necessary. One surprise is that near the summit the hiker comes upon the Vallecito de Lilis, apparently named after the 19th century dictator Ulises Heureaux, undoubtedly one of very few places which still commemorates his reign. The summit of Pico Duarte provides a panoramic view of the surrounding countryside. Local people claim that Trujillo visited Pico Duarte and changed the name to Pico Trujillo, just as he changed Santo Domingo's name to Ciudad Trujillo. In neither case did Trujillo's name remain in place after his assassination.

Living in the remote forest in this high peak area are the hutia, a small rodent native to the area, and the wild boar (which was originally brought from Europe). There are lots of hummingbirds along the trail. Other birds characteristic of the park are the: Hispaniolan woodpecker, white-necked crow, palm chat, Hispaniolan trogon, ruddy quail dove, red-tailed hawk, Antillean siskin, rufous-throated solitaire, loggerhead flycatcher, red-necked pigeon, black swift, green-tailed warbler and mourning dove.

Appendix A

List of Hotels

The hotel list corresponds to the text and includes information needed to find each hotel. Relative prices are indicated by using the price of a double room at the time of writing:

L —luxury $100+
E —expensive $50–$100
M—moderate $20–$50
C —cheap $20–

AC—Airconditioning T   —Tennis
TV—Television   Ja —Jacuzzi
R —Restaurant   Sa —Sauna
D —Dico/Nightclub   HR —Horsebackriding
E —Entertainment   Go —Golf
Ca —Casino   BaSi—Babysitting
P —Pool

Note: a number of hotels listed here in the (C) category are quite basic, rarely have foreign guests, do not have English speaking staff and would not be suitable for many travelers. Hotels which are particularly recommended by the authors are marked with "∗."

Chapter 4

Luperon
Luperon Beach Resort (L), 581-4153 or 685-0151, fax 809-581-6262, remote (see text), AC,TV,R,D,P,T,Ja,BaSi, ∗

Monte Cristi

Las Caravelas (C), 579-2682, 19 rooms; this rustic hotel is located on the road out of town toward El Morro (see text) and the ocean; visitors need their own transportation.

Hotel Chic (C), 579-2316, C. Moncion; this basic hotel is located near the center of town with local restaurants and bars nearby.

Dajabon

Juan Calvo (C), 579-8285, C. Henriquez

Rosario (C), 579-8477, C. Henriquez

Puerto Plata

Puerto Plata Beach Resort (L), 586-4243, fax (809) 586-4377, Ave Malecon, 216 rooms, AC,TV,R,D,E,P,T,*

Caracol (C), 586-2588, Malecon, 52 rooms

Castilla (C), 586-2559, JF Kennedy, 7 rooms

Condado (C), 586-3255, Av. Justo, 25 rooms

Guaronia (C), 586-2109, Av. 12 de Julio, 12 rooms

Ilra (C), 586-2337, Villanueva, 8 rooms

Imperial (C), 586-1440, Villanueva, 13 rooms

Montemar (M), 586-2800, Av. Luperon, 95 rooms, R,D,P,T,

Mountain View (M), 586-5757, Av. Kunhardt, 22 rooms

Hostal Jimesson (M), 586-5131, John F. Kennedy, 22 rooms, AC,R

Costambar (3 km. from Puerto Plata)

Bayside Hill Beach Resort (L), 535-3149 or 586-5260, fax (809) 586-5545, C. Guayacanes corner Bermejo, 150 rooms, AC,TV,R,D,E,P,T,Go,Ja,BR

Apart Hotel Marlena (M), 586-3692, 33 studios w/kitchen

Cofresi (M), 586-2898, 192 rooms AC,R,D,E,P,T,HR,

Apart Hotel Atlantis (L), Calle Principal S/N, 586-3828, fax (809) 586-4276, 63 rooms, AC,TV,R,P,T,Go

Playa Dorada (see map, east of Puerto Plata)
All Playa Dorado Hotels are of the upper price class (E or L), have direct beach access, a common golf course. All rooms provide AC,TV, R, P,E, T (excpt. Heavens)

Villas Doradas (L), (809) 533-2131, in US 1-800-457-0067, fax (809) 532-5306 or (809) 586-4790, 207 rooms

Jack Tar Village (L), (809) 586-3800, in US 1-800-527-9299, fax (809) 586-4161, 300 rooms, D,E, Ca, BaSi,Ja,Sa, *

Playa Dorado Hotel (L), (809) 586-3988, fax (809) 586-1190, 253 rooms, D,Ca

Eurohotel Beach Resort (E), (809) 586-3663, fax (809) 586-4858, 40 rooms, D,Ca

Hotel Playa Dorada Princess (E), (809) 320-5350, fax (809) 320-5386, 336 rooms, D

Dorado Naco Beach Resort (L), (809) 586-2019, fax (809) 586-3608, 202 rooms, D,Ca

Village Caraibe (E), (809) 586-4811, fax (809) 533-6212, 208 rooms

Heavens (L), (809) 586-5250, fax (809) 346-2045, 150 rooms

Victoria Resort (L), (809) 586-1200, fax (809) 586-4862, 120 rooms

Sosua
Atlantic (M), 571-2707, Av. Martinez, 10 rooms

Apart Hotel One Ocean Place (M), 571-3131, fax (809) 571-3144, 50 apts., AC,TV,R,P

Sand Castle Beach Resort (L), 571-2420, fax 571-2000, located northwest of town on ocean, easy access to public beach, good dining options, 240 rooms, AC,TV,R,D,E,P,T,BR

El Paraiso Hotel (M), 571-2906, C. Rosen

Elena's Hotel (M), 571-2872, C. Llibre

Hostal de Lora (M), 571-3939, Av Martinez, 32 rooms, R,P,Ja

Koch's Guest House, 571-2284, off Av. Martinez (see text) 11 rooms, good value, run by one of the original German-Jewish settlers

La Posada (M), 571-2235, Av. Kunhardt

Los Almendros (E), 78 rooms, 571-3530, main road by turnoff for El Batey, AC,TV,R,D,E,Ja

Montana (C), 53 rooms, 571-2255, C. Llibre, 64 rooms, R,P

Palm Resort (M), 69 rooms, 571-3686, C. Ana Maria

Paradise Coralillos (M), 26 rooms, 571-2645, Av. Martinez, R,P, beach access

Paradise Villas Larimar (E), 75 rooms, 571-2367, Av. Martinez

Sea Breeze (E), 30 rooms, 571-3858, Av. Martinez, near synagogue (see text)

Sir Francis Drake (E), 109 rooms, 571-3850, C. Norte, 109 rooms, AC,TV,R,D,E,P,Ja,HR

Solimar (M), 14 rooms, 571-3303, Av. Kunhardt

Sosua (M), 36 rooms, 571-2683, Ave Martinez, Ac,R,P, good value, pleasant pool and ambiance, good meals, *

Tiburon Blanco (M), 20 rooms, 571-3471, C. Rosen, R,P

Vista Mar (E), 50 rooms, 571-3000, Los Cerros

Sosua Paradise Resort (E), 571-3438, Av. Martinez, 28 rooms, AC,TV,R,E,P,Ja,BR,HR

Sosua by the Sea (M), 111 rooms, 571-3222, fax (809) 571-3020, Av. Martinez, AC,TV,R,P,Ja,BR

Sosua Caribbean Fantasy (L), 571-2534, 68 rooms, AC,TV,R,D,P,Ja

Playa Chiquita (M), 90 rooms, 571-2800, along Hwy, AC,TV,R,P,T

Cabarete
Auberge du Roi Tropical (M), 29 rooms, 571-0770, along Hwy

Cabarete Beach Hotel (M), 18 rooms, 571-0755

Cabarete Palm Beach Condos (M), 571-0758, fax (809) 571-0752, along Hwy

Las Orqidias (M), 36 rooms, 571-0787

Voile O Berge (M), 30 rooms, 571-0879

Windsurf Aparthotel (M), 35 rooms, 571-0710

Cabarete Beach Resort (M), 571-0833

Punta Goleta Beach Resort (E), 132 rooms, 571-0700, fax (809) 581-3496, AC,TV,R,D,P,T,HR, *

Camino del Sol (E), 75 rooms, 571-2858, AC,TV,R,P,T,Ja,BR

Rio San Juan
Rio San Juan (M), 38 rooms, 589-2379, C. Duarte, large pool, good meals (see text), functional rooms without screens, R,P

La Bahia Blanca (M), 589-2562, C.Deligne (see text), on beach, sea breeze and good view, C. Deligne (see text), R, *

Santa Clara (C), 14 rooms, 589-2286, C. Billini

Chapter 5

Nagua
Caban-Carib (M), 16 rooms, 543-6420, fax 584-3145, on beach, east of town on main road toward Samana, individual cabin rates vary depending on view and mosquito nets, far from other tourist resorts, excellent food (see text), Austrian management, *

El Sol Naciente (C), 10 rooms, 584-2211, C. Minaya

Oasis (C), 42 rooms, 584-2434, C. Minaya

Las Terrenas (all hotels are on the beach)
Acaya (M), on Punta Bonita (see text), 8 rooms

Punta Bonita Beach Hotel (M), 567-9575 in S.D. on Punta Bonita, 21 rooms, R

Atlantis (E), 589-9300, on Punta Bonita, 10 rooms, German management, R

Punta Bonita Cabanas (M), 589-9309, on Punta Bonita, *

Isla Bonita (M), 562-6209, 8 rooms, good food, pleasant ambiance, Italian management, *

La Louisiana (C), 4 rooms, reasonably priced meals

Tropical Banana (E), 589-9410, 25 rooms, relaxed ambiance, R,P

Cacao Beach Resort (E), 589-9589, 191 rooms, AC,TV,R, D,E,P,T,HR,BR

El Portillo Beach Club (L), 687-9157 in S.D., 99 rooms, east of Làs Terrenas, all inclusive, vast beach, AC,TV,R,D, E,P,T,HR,BR, *

Samana
Hostal Cotuabanama (M), 15 rooms, 538-2557, round building, C. Sanchez

Cayacoa Beach Resort (M), 538-2426, (see text), 66 rooms, good view, causeway out onto Samana bay, AC,TV,R,D,P, nearby beach

Tropical Lodge (M), 538-2480, Ave Marina, 8 rooms, good value along Malecon toward Las Galevas, easy access to docks for whale watching and restaurants, good food, French Canadian management, *

King Hotel (C), 10 rooms, no screens, on left before turnoff for Cayacoa, basic

Bay Resort Gran Bahia (L), exclusive, 562-6271, fax (809) 562-5232, Los Cacaos, 98 rooms, AC,TV,R,D,E,P,T, beach access, trips to Cayo Levantado and whale watching, on road north toward Las Galeras, *

Las Galeras
Moorea Beach (M), can only be contacted via fax (809) 538-2545 or 689-4105, only hotel at Las Galeras, 12 rooms, boats and horses available, French management, *

Chapter 6

Santiago
Matum (M), 581-3107, near monument (see text), 50 rooms, AC,R,D,P,Ca

Santiago Camino Real (M), 581-7000, C. El Sol, 72 rooms, AC,TV,R,D, good hotel in mid-town location, excellent view from restaurant, classy and popular disco.

Ambar (C), 575-1957, Av. Sadhala, AC,TV,R,D,E

Don Diego (C), 575-4186, Av. Sadhala, 36 rooms

San Francisco de Macoris
Macoris (C), 588-2350, Av. Restauracion

Nuevo Central (C), 588-2304, C. San Francisco

Olimpico (C), 588-3584, Av. Libertad

San Jose de las Matas
La Mansion (M), 270 rooms (including cabins), 581-0395, fax
(809) 581-9085, good value, great view (see text), R,D,P,Ja, *

Buenos Aires (C), 578-8354, on main road entering town

Chapter 7

San Cristobal
San Cristobal (C), 12 rooms, 528-3555, Av. Libertad

Constitucion (C), 528-3309, Av. Constitucion

Bani
Alba (C), 522-3590, C. Billini

Caribani (C), 522-4400, across from town hall

Las BBB (C), 522-4422, on main road

Silvia (C), 522-4674, on main road

San Jose de Ocoa
Rancho Francisco (M), 558-2291, south of town on main road, decent accommodations in a romote part of the country

Elias (C), 558-2627, Las Carreras

Azua
Altagracia (C), 521-3286, C. Duarte

Brisas del Mar (C), 521-3813, C. de Leones

Ramon (C), 521-3529 on main road

Barahona
Guarocuya (C), 524-2211, good value, on beach, 23 rooms, (see text)

Caribe (C), 524-2185, good value, across from Guarocuya, 25 rooms

Swiss Hotel (C), 10 km. south of Barahona

Pedernales
Noruega (c), 524-0152, C. Libertad

Pension Familiar Hugria (C), 524-0144, C. Libertad

San Juan de la Maguana
Maguana (M), 24 rooms, 577-2244, right by arch (see text chapter 7), although somewhat rundown, it is the best hotel for at least 50 miles in any direction. R,P

Tamarindo (C), 557-2256, across from Maguana

Chapter 8

Santo Domingo

Jaragua (L), 686-2222, Av George Washington 367, 355 rooms, recently bought by the Ramada Hotel Group, situated on 14 acres of beautifully landscaped land along the ocean, ten stories high, all rooms have magnificent views, very spacious rooms are tastefully decorated, have marble bathrooms equipped with hairdryers and additional small TVs, AC,TV,R,D,E,P,T,Ja,Sa,Ca,BaSi, *

Embajador (L), 533-2131, Av. Sarasota, 316 rooms, located in the western part of town, elegant lobby and shopping arcade, rooms facing south have ocean views, are spacious with traditional decor, landscaped gardens create a club-like relaxing atmosphere around open cafeteria and pool, AC,TV,R,D,E,P,T,Sa,BaSi, *

Plaza Naco (E), 562-3100, Av. Tiradentes 22, 217 rooms, mid-town location, close to Plaza Naco shopping mall, rooms have kitchenettes, AC,TV,R,D,E,Ca,P,Sa,BaSi

Hispaniola (E), 535-7111, Av. Independencia, 165 rooms, business oriented clientele, the same management as the Santo Domingo Hotel across the street, guests are entitled to use facilities of the sister hotel, rooms are comfortable, but only a few have a seaside view, impressive casino, AC,TV,R,D,E,Ca,P,BaSi

Lina (E), 686-5000, Av. M. Gomez, 220 rooms, mid-town hotel recently renovated. Modern and comfortable rooms, but lacking in tropical ambiance, AC,TV,R,D,E,Ca,P,T,Sa,BaSi

Napolitano (M), 687-1131, Av. G. Washington, 73 rooms, located on the Malecon within walking distance to the colonial zone, functional rooms, some with ocean view, AC,TV,R,D,P,

Santo Domingo (L), 535-1511, Av. Independencia, 220 rooms, elegant city hotel along the ocean with interiors designed by Oscar de la Renta, rooms are very comfortable and well set up, fourteen acres of tropical greenery surround the hotel, AC,TV,R,D,E,P,T,Sa,BaSi,*

Sheraton (L), 688-0823, Av. G. Washington, 260 rooms, business oriented hotel conveniently located along the ocean, lacks an appealing facade, rooms above the 3rd floor have ocean view, AC,TV,R,D,E,Ca,P,T,BaSi,

Fiesta (L), 562-8222, Av. Anacaona, 316 rooms, recently changed owners and is trying to live up to its 5-star reputation, located on the edge of town. Transportation can be difficult, often hosts conventions, rooms are comfortable and spacious, and some have ocean views, AC,TV,R,D,E,Ca,P,T,Sa

Delta (M), 535-9722, Av. Sarasota 53, 67 rooms, AC,TV,R,D,E,Ja

Hostal Palacio Nicolas de Ovando (E), 687-3101, Calle Las Damas, 55 rooms, excellent location for sight seers in the heart of the colonial zone (see text) right near the Alcazar, AC,TV,R,P,*

Cervantes (M), 686-8161, Av. Cervantes 202, 180 rooms, centrally located within walking distance to Malecon, rooms are functional and clean, good value, good and reasonably priced restaurant, AC,TV,R,D,P,Sa,*

Commodoro (M), 687-7141, Av. Bolivar 193, 90 rooms, centrally located, disco on first floor, quiet rooms on upper floors, small but clean rooms, good value, AC,TV,R,D,E,P,BaSi

Commercial (C), 682-8161, El Conde 201, 75 rooms, central downtown location, basic but clean, good value for budget oriented traveler, restaurant not recommended, AC,TV,R,D

Hotel Caribe 1 (E), 688-8141, fax 688-8149, Av. Maximo Gomez, 42 rooms, family style conveniently located,
AC,TV,R,D,P

Hotel San Geronimo (M), 533-8181, Av. Independencia 1067,
72 rooms, conveniently located, functional hotel, small basic
rooms, some kitchenettes, AC,TV,R,Ca,P

Apart Hotels in Santo Domingo
Apart Hotels are a good option for visitors staying more than just
a few days. They include room service, have kitchenettes and
charge by the week or month.

Apart Hotel Naco (M), 541-6226, Av. Tirandentes, 108 units,
centrally located, close to the Plaza Naco shopping mall,
AC,TV,R,P,D,E

Apart Hotel Drake (M), 567-4427, Augustin Lara 29, 28 apts.,
located in an affluent residential neighborhood close to the Plaza
Naco shopping mall, AC,TV,R,

Apart Hotel Aladino (M), 567-0144, H.Pieter 34, 21 units, Naco
area, modestly furnished and equipped

Apart Hotel Plaza del Sol (M), 687-1317, Jose Contreras 25-A,
23 units, conveniently located with ocean view from top floor,
studios are fully equipped, cafeteria services

Apart Hotel Plaza Florida (M), 541-3650 Av. Bolivar 203, 32
units, centrally located, first floor of the building is occupied by
shops while the two upper floors comprise the hotel, spacious
one bedroom apartments, comfortably furnished, AC,TV

Apart Hotel Plaza Colonial (M), 687-9111, C.O. Pellerano cor-

ner Julio Verne, 160 units, centrally located, one and two bedroom apartments

Chapter 9

Boca Chica
Boca Chica Beach Resort (E), 523-4333 or 523-4521, C. 20 de
Deciembre, 191 rooms, includes food, trip to nearby island,
AC,TV,R,D,E,P,T, *

Marena Beach Resort (E), 567-9575, 100 rooms,
AC,TV,R,D,P,T

Sun Set Beach Resort (M), 523-4580 or 535-4606, C. Duarte,
70 rooms, AC,TV,R, D,E,P,HR

Don Juan Beach Resort (E), 682-9080, fax (809) 688-5271, 111
rooms, AC,TV,R,D,E,P,T

Caney (C), 523-4314, 17 rooms, C. Duarte

El Cheveron (C), 523-4333, 7 rooms, C. Duarte, AC,R

Juan Dolio and Guayacanes (Playas del Este)
Talanquera Hotel (E), 688-6604 or 526-1510, 275 rooms,
AC,TV,R,D,E,P,T,Sa,Ja,BR

Villas del Mar (M), 30 rooms, 529-3735

Punta Garza (E), 533-2131, 144 rooms, AC,TV,R,D

Playa Real (E), 526-1114, fax 526-1013, 56 rooms,
AC,R,P,T,HR,BR

Costa Linda (M), 526-3011, 166 rooms, AC,R,P,BR

Decameron (L), 223-9815 or 526-2307, along Hwy, 288 rooms, AC,TV,R,D,E,Ca,P,T,BR, casino

Metro Hotel (E), 526-1710, fax 526-1808, 174 rooms, 72 apts, good value, reef just off beach front, comfortable rooms, some with balconies and ocean view, avoid rooms close to the pool if you go to bed early, AC,R,D,E,P,T,BR, *

Embassy Beach Resort (M), 526-2027, along Hwy, 96 rooms, AC,TV,R,P,BR

Tamarindo Sun Resort (E), 526-1410, main road, AC,TV,R,P,BR

San Pedro de Macoris
Macorix (M), 529-3950, along Malecon, 28 rooms, probably the best hotel in town, AC,R,P

America (C), 529-2349, C. de Garza

Brisa del Caribe (C), 526-8956, C. Rojas

Buffant (C), 526-6983, C. 10 de Septiembre

Dafni (C), 529-4040, C. Toconal

Royal (C), 529-7105, C. Castillo

Sabana de la Mar
Villa Suiza (C), 556-7304, C. Moncion, on shore east side of town, 14 rooms, beautiful view of Samana Bay, no screens, can arrange for trip to Los Haitises National Park, probably the best hotel in town, R,P

Brisas de la Bahia (C), 556-7318, C. Duarte

Don Quijote (C), 556-7236, Av. de los Heroes

La Romana
Cabanas Tio Tom (M), 556-6211, on the right entering town from Santo Domingo before turnoff for Higuey, 72 rooms, basic accommodations but clean, reasonable restaurant, decent pool, AC,R,P,*

Frano (C), 21 rooms, on main road into town

Libra Apart Hotel (M), 556-3787, C. Gil number 11, AC,TV,Ki

Condado (C), 556-3010, C. Altagracia, 24 rooms

Casa de Campo (L), in U.S. 1-800-223-6620, 682-2111, on far side of the Dulce River, covers 7,000 acres, sandy beach (Las Minitas), 750 luxurious rooms, yachting facilities, 13 clay tennis courts (10 lighted), 19 swimming pools, two 18-hole golf courses (one along the ocean), hundreds of horses and polo (October through May), trail riding, skeet shooting, innumerable aquatic sports, very exclusive, (see text),*

Altos de Chavon
La Posada Inn (L), call Casa de Campo for reservations, 10 rooms, AC,P, (see text)

Bayahibe
Bayahibe (M), 10 rustic rooms, no hot water, good value, generator

Tranquera (C), rustic cabins, no hot water

Dominicus Beach Village Resort (L), 689-8720, 886-5658, 129 basic rooms, rustic decor, all inclusive, situated on 3,000 acres of vast and solitary beach (see text), avoid rooms close to the pool if you go to bed early, R,E,P,T,BR,*

Higuey
Ana (C), 544-3569, C. Hijo

Brisas del Este (C), 554-2312, 18 rooms, C. Mella

Colon (C), 554-4283, C. Colon

Don Carlos (C), 554-2344, C. Ponce de Leon

Genisis (C), 554-2971, C. Colon

La Hora (C), 554-2603, C. Adamanay

Las Campanas (C), 554-2675, C. Arzobispo Nouel

Punta Cana
Club Med (L), 687-2767 or 567-5220 (S.D.), all inclusive, 105 acres, 340 rooms, traditional Club Med ambiance and nightlife (see text), AC,R,D,E,P,T,BaSi,BR

Punta Cana Beach Resort (L), 686-0084 or 541-2114 (S.D) fax 687-8745, 246 rooms, all inclusive, excellent value and entertainment, good food and vast beaches (see text), AC,TV,R,E, E,P,T,HR,BaSi,BR,*

Bavaro Beach (L), 1,349 rooms, 686-5797 or 685-8411 (in S.D.), fax (809) 686-5859, huge and well managed hotel complex (see text), all inclusive with lots of choices, AC,TV, R,D,E,Ca,P,T,HR,BR,*

Chapter 10

Constanza
Swiss Chalet (C), 62 rooms, 539-2233, despite gorgeous location not recommended at the time of writing (see text)

Mi Cabana (C), 539-2472, C. Rufino Espinosa, 18 rooms, probably the best hotel in town (see text)

Margarita (C), 539-2269, C. Luperon

Brisas del Valle (C), 539-2365, C. Gratereaux

Jarabacoa

Hotel de La Montana (M), 27 rooms, located on the outskirts of Jarabacoa coming from the Autopista Duarte, beautiful view and impressive structure (see text), billiards available, large rooms, R,P

La Ganja Guest House (C), across from Hotel de la Montana

Hotel Pinar Dorado (M), 77 rooms, on the edge of town along the road to Constanza, 574-2820, good restaurant and screens on the windows, R, P, horse rentals outsede (see text), *

Manabao

Patria Muñoz (C), very rustic, only should be used by hikers enroute to Pico Duarte (see text)

Appendix B

Dominican Cuisine

Dominican food (*comida criolla*) is enjoyable but not elaborate. Rice and beans are a staple and are called *moro* when mixed together or *la bandera dominicana* (the Dominican flag) when combined with meat. *Tostones* (sliced fried plantains) often accompany a main dish in place of *papas fritas* (French fries). Plantains are an essential part of Dominican cooking and are fried, boiled or mashed. Although they strongly resemble bananas (which are also widely available), plantains cannot be eaten unless they are cooked. Mashed green plantains fried with onions, known as *mangu*, is a common Dominican breakfast. Lots of melons are grown in the desert-like Azua area, ranging from cantelopes to watermelons. A Dominican specialty is *sancocho*, a stew of chicken or meat cooked with yucca and plantains, seasoned with pepper, coriander and a dash of vinegar. Pork (*cerdo*) and goat (*chivo*) dishes are popular. Other local favorites include *chicharron de cerdo* or *de pollo*, which are deep fried pork or chicken skins. Sausages, such as the *chorizo* (a beef sausage), *longaniza* (a spicy pork sausage similar to an Italian sausage), or *morcilla* (a blood sausage) are much enjoyed.

The wide variety of different climatic zones in the Dominican Republic are responsible for a wealth of local fruits. Pineapples, *pina*, are native to the island and excellent fruits are available year round. The passion fruit, *chinola*, is an egg-sized fruit ranging in color from yellow to purple which makes an excellent juice (its name comes from the Spaniards who said the plant's

dramatic white and purple color reminded them of Christ's cru-
cifixion). Excellent mangoes are available from May to August
(the larger the better they taste). Fresh grapefruits and oranges
are available everywhere for a pittance. Papaya *(lechosa)* is available year round and is popular with breakfast or as a dessert (and
is an effective meat tenderizer). The *mamoncillo, mamon,* and
especially the delicious *mamey* (which looks a bit like a rough
skinned grapefruit and has a large pit) are fruits unfamiliar to
most English speakers and should be sampled. *Guayabe* (guava)
is a yellow to green fruit with a strong fragrance which is used
for juices and marmalade. Other fruits used primarily for juices
are the *tamarindo, nispero, jagua,* and *guanabana.* The *zapote*
is a rough skinned brown fruit used primarily for milk shakes
and ice cream.

Dominican desserts tend to be very sweet, not surprising considering how much sugar is produced locally. Enjoyable desserts
include *tres leches* (a rich cake with creamy frosting), *biscocho
con suspiro* (a cake with a meringue cream), *palitos de coco* (a
coconut cake) *majarete* (corn pudding).

List of Restaurants

Prices (full meal per person):

F.—expensive   US$30+
M—moderate   US$15–30
R —reasonable   US$5–15

Restaurants particularly recommended by the authors are marked
by *.

Chapter 4

Puerto Plata
Los Pinos (E), Av. Hermanas Mirabal, 586-3222, good steaks,
vegetables and lobster, *comida criolla*

Roma II (M), Calle Beller No. 45, 586-3904, Italian and Spanish, excellent food and service, *

El Espanol (M), Av. Circunvalacion Sur, 586-1655, Spanish and International

De Armando (E), A.Mota 23, 586-3418, excellent Italian food in an elegant yet homey style, large variety of soups and seafood specialties (e.g., delicious "Lobster Atlantic" in a house sauce); try the typical Dominican desert *majarete* or the *cocoyuca*, a yuca flan with coconut; reservations advisable, *

Pizzeria Roma II (R), Beller, 586-3904, casual setting overlooking central park, Italian specialties at good prices

Valter's (E), C.Hermanas Mirabal, 586-2329, beautiful setting in a Victorian-style house, menu emphasizes seafood and Italian specialties, good service, *

Neptune Bar & Grill (E), Puerto Plata Beach Resort, 586-4243, perfect site to enjoy fish and seafood in a setting along the ocean; menu includes lots of seafood and meat, open for lunch and dinner from 12pm to 11pm, *

La Isabela (E), Hotel Montemar, Malecon, 586-2800, seafood and steak specialties, with a large variety of desserts

Jimmy's (E), Calle Beller 72, 586-4325, very popular restaurant with seafood and beef specialties, reservations advisable, *

Sosua
Leandro's (M), Carretera Cabarete 3, 571-0713, *comida criolla*

Oasis (M), Dr. A. Martinez, El Batey, 571-2288, *comida criolla*

Morua Mai (E), C.P.Clisante, El Batey, 571-2503, excellent seafood, good service, *

Lorenzo's (R), Calle P. Clisante, El Batey, 571-2568, Italian specialties at good prices

On the Waterfront (M), 571-3024, built next to lookout point down from the phone company office, folk bands and live music, variety of good food, breakfast, lunch and dinner, *

Marco Polo (M), Dr. Alejo Martinez, 571-2445, dining with an excellent view of Sosua Bay, good food, *

De Armando (M), C.P. Clisante, 571-3022, recently opened sister restaurant of same name in Puerto Plata, Italian specialties

Da Albert (M), Dr. A. Martinez, 571-2069, Italian and international menu

Pollo Rico, C.P.Clisante (R), El Batey, 571-2445, cafeteria style eating (almost fast food), chicken a good value

Chapter 5

Las Terrenas
Hotel Atlantis (E), (see text for directions), 589-9300, Good food and pleasant ambiance, outside dining with breeze from the nearby ocean, live music, German management

Isla Bonita Restaurant (M), Italian, connected with the hotel of the same name, pleasant seaside ambiance and very good food, *

La Louisiana (R), French and international at very reasonable prices

Tropical Banana (E), 589-9410

Samana
Julio Hung Boite (R), C. T. Chasereux, 538-2215, Chinese, good view of Samana Bay, overlooking La Churcha (see text), generous portions, outside option, food good but not gourmet

La Mata Rosada (E), Malecon 5, 538-2215, along Malecon, food good but portions are not large

Cafe de Paris (M), Malecon 6, excellent food, pleasant and very informal atmosphere, *

El Nautico (E), good seafood along Malecon, 538-2587

El Bucanero (M), along Malecon directly over main dock, sea breeze, live music.

Le France (M), very good food, pleasant ambiance, along Malecon, French management, *

La Hacienda (M), 538-2383, good food, French management, just off Malecon near center of town

Hotel Gran Bahia (E), good food in luxurious atmosphere and great ocean view, dining inside or on the terrace

Las Galeras
Martinique (M), good food, French management

Jardin Tropical (M), good food, informal

Chapter 6

Santiago
Rositania (M), 582-2518, Av. Juan Pablo Duarte 28, *comida criolla*

El Hidalgo (E), 581-7000, Hotel Camino Real, Calle del Sol, formal restaurant located on top of the building houses Camino Real Hotel in downtown Santiago and affords excellent view of city, very good food and service, *

Pez Dorado (R), Chinese, 582-2518, Calle del Sol 43

Monumental (R), Chinese, 583-1894, Calle Beller 1

Pizzeria Roma (M), Italian, 582-8603, Av. J.P. Duarte 72

Roma (M), Italian and Spanish, Av. Juan Pablo Duarte, 582-8603, great pasta and meat dishes, wide selection of imported wines, *

El Sol (M), Italian, 583-0767, Calle del Sol

Chapter 7

San Cristobal
Terraza Paso Fino (R), 528-4220, Av. Constitucion

Cafeteria Pico Pollo (R), 528-2882, specializing in chicken, Av. Maria Trinidad Sanchez 9B

Bani
Pizzaria Mi Estancia (R), Italian, pizzas and basic meals, outside or inside seating available, on main road near town square, Calle Mella 33

Azua
Patio Espanol El Jardin (R), 521-2224, Calle Duarte 49

Barahona
La Rocca (R), 524-2544, restaurant covered open air, good food and service, directly across from Hotel Guaracuyo (see text) sea

breeze, portions large, connected to Hotel Caribe, generator works when power fails, *

Brisas del Mar (R), Chinese, along Malecon (see text), excellent food, large portions and good view of the bay, *

Chapter 8

Santo Domingo
MEXICAN
Antojito (M), Av. Lope de Vega 49, 567-1118

ITALIAN
Pitiri (E), Calle Nicolas de Bari No. 6, just off Tiradentes between Bolivar and Nicolas Pension, 541-5478, extensive menu including many desserts, excellent shrimp, steaks and lobster, *

Il Buco, (E), Arzobispo Merino 152 A, 685-0884, very popular restaurant in the colonial zone, homemade pasta and fabulous seafood, *

Vesuvius I, (E), Av. G. Washington 521, 682-2766, on the Malecon, indoor or outdoors with a view of the ocean, international cuisine to pastas, live lobster sold by weight, *

Vesuvius II, (E), Av. Tiradentes 17, 562-6060, somewhat less decorative atmosphere than Vesuvio I, same good food in quieter setting

La Piazetta (M), located in Hotel Hispaniola, 532-1511

Italiano Milano (R), Dr. Baez 23, in Gascue area near National Palace, 682-4397, excellent homemade pastas, *

Figaro (E), located in the Hotel Jaragua, 686-2222, good food and service

SPANISH

Don Pepe (M), Pasteur 41, 689-7612, excellent steak and Spanish foods, good service, *

El Alcazar (E), located in the Hotel Santo Domingo, 532-1511, good food and excellent service.

El Bodegon (M), Padre Billini corner Avenida Merino, small and cozy, in the colonial zone, lunch and dinner, good soups and Spanish delicacies, 682-6864

Extremadura (M), located inside Hostal Nicolas de Ovando in Calle Las Damas, good food, great ambiance and convenient location for exploring colonial zone, 687-3101

El Mason de Castilla (E), Dr. Baez 8, 688-4319, good food, imperial ambitions

Reina de Espana (E), Calle Cervantes 103, 685-2588, good food

Iberia, (R), Miguel Angel Monclus 165, 530-7200, off beaten path and not easy to find, but worth the search. Driving west on 27 de Febrero turn left (south) at the traffic light on Calle Privada just past Nunez de Caceres; a private house without a sign, closed Monday, superb home-style cooking, no printed menu, owner recommends what's fresh. *

FRENCH

Cafe St. Michel (E), Av. Lope de Vega 24, 562-4141, not very elegant but comfortable setting, food excellent and basically Caribbean with constantly changing menus; on Fridays and Saturdays try the "menu de degustacion," which permits trying small portions of 8 different kinds of food, open for lunch and dinner, *

La Fromagerie (E), Plaza Criolla, 567-8606, Av. 27 de Febrero, excellent food and service, *

Le Cafe, (M), Av. G. Washington, 687-3982, casual eatery with outdoor terrace overlooking the Malecon, light meals and excellent desserts

Antoine's, (E), Hotel Sheraton, 685-1413, good food in elegant atmosphere

Maison de Bari (M), Calle Hostos, this excellent bar and restaurant is favorite with local artist and intellectual types in colonial zone (see text), pleasant and informal ambiance, seating limited, wonderful steaks, *

CHINESE
Salon de Te (M), just down steps from Alcazar and across from La Ataranza museum (see text), excellent food and decor, ideal location, *

Gran Muralla, (M), 27 de Febrero 218, 567-2166, huge multi-level restaurant, very popular for midday brunch on Sundays

Jardin de Jade (E), inside Hotel Embajador, 533-2131, Av. Sarasota, elegant oriental restaurant elaborately decorated, Mandarin, Cantones and Sechuan specialties, *

Lee's Kitchen (M), Mejia Ricart 64, 544-1862, informal Chinese setting, generous portions, takeout available, *

Mario's, No. 299, 27 de Febrero near Winston Churchill, excellent sweet and sour pork, steaks and seafood, *

Lotus (E), located inside Hotel Jaragua, 686-2222, Av. G. Washington

SEAFOOD
Juan Carlos (E), G.M. Ricart 7, 562-6444, sumptuous ambiance, excellent food and service, *

Jai Alai, (M), Av. Independencia 411, 685-2409, informal setting with outdoor and indoor dining, live guitar music on evenings, specialty is seafood with a Peruvian flavor

La Mesquita (M), Av. Independencia 407, 687-7090, good food and pleasant ambiance

COMIDA CRIOLLA
Fonda La Atarazana, (M), Atarazana 5, 685-2409, located in colonial zone in a restored building; at night musicians perform in the interior courtyard.

Meson de la Cava (E), Av. Mirador del Sur, 533-2818. Eating in this restaurant is a real adventure because it is an underground cave; food and service are excellent and the experience is unforgettable, specializes in beef dishes, located in Mirador del Sur (see text) not far from the huge underground disco, *

Maniqui (R), located in Plaza de la Cultura near the art museum, meals can be taken inside or out, excellent Dominican food and ambiance (service is not rapid), 687-6621, *

VEGETARIAN
Ojas (R), Jonas Salk 2, near the corner of Independencia, two blocks west of Maximo Gomez, 682-3940, good plantain, bean and rice dishes, excellent desserts, *

Ananda (R), Casimiro de Moya 7, 682-4465, Gascue area two blocks east of Cervantes and south of Calle Santiago, unique restaurant connected with yoga group serves generous portions of great vegetarian food in an almost mystical ambiance, cafteria-style (Point at what you want), excellent lentil dishes and pastries, *

ARGENTINE
Asadero los Argentinos (M), No. 809 Independencia at the corner of Maximo Gomez, 686-7060 or 688-6792, steaks

Chapter 9

Boca Chica
Bambu (R), Chinese, 523-4828, San Rafael 10-A

Piccola (R), Italian, 523-4620, Calle Duarte 36

San Pedro de Macoris
Portofino (R), Italian, 526-6107, Av. Malecon

Pizzeria La Roca (R), Italian, 529-3069, Av. Malecon 9

Hotel Macorix (R), *comida criolla*, 529-3950, on the Malecon
in the town's largest hotel, Deligne

La Romana
La Casita (M), Italian, Francisco Richiez Docoudry No. 57,
556-5509, excellent food, located on the west side of the Dulce
river (see text), Italian management, *

El Huerto (R), *comida criolla*, 573-4348, Jose Rodriguez on the
corner of Moya

Don Quijote's (R), on Parque Duarte (the town's central square)

Casa de Campo
Tropicana (E), seafood and Chinese, 523-3333

Lago Grill (E), *comida criolla*, 523-3333

Altos de Chavon
La Pizzella (M), Italian, restaurant on platform, popular with a
young crowd, good pizza

El Sombrero (E), Mexican, good food, near the center of village, *

La Fonda (E), Spanish, good food and pleasant ambiance

Cafteria La Casa (M), reliably good food

Casa del Rio (E), French, beautiful view of the Chavon River, excellent food, *

Higuey
El Gran Gourmet (R), good food and drink, tends to be over airconditioned, near La Basilica (see text), *

Bayahibe
Tamarinde (R), all restaurants in this small town are within easy walking distance of each other and reasonably priced, ideal for the budget traveler, on the ocean with a great view

La Tanquera (R), in modest hotel of same name, basic meals in a rustic setting

Bayahibe (R), right on ocean, good and inexpensive food

Bahia (R), good but simple food

Chapter 10

Constanza
Lorenzo's (R), probably the best restaurant in Constanza, informal atmosphere and good steaks and chicken, bar (see text)

Jarabacoa
Hotel de la Montana (R), restaurant in hotel on the road from Autopista Duarte in the outskirts of town, 685-8025, great view in daylight of the pine covered mountains, food good but service slow

Dorado de Pinar (M), food and service good, occasional foreign tourists, barbecue is good deal, *

Appendix C

Merengue

The origin of *merengue* is shrouded in mystery. Although some historians attempt to trace its antecedents to the Taino or the pirates on Tortuga Island, most agree it resulted from a fusion of African rhythm and Spanish melody. Basic similarities have been detected to Spanish flamenco dancing. Merengue music and dance first emerged as a major cultural force among the rural peasantry in the Cibao area (near Santiago) to the chagrin of local landowners who tended to prefer more traditional Spanish music. The earliest comprehensive written report on merengue was an article in a Dominican newspaper called "El Oasis" in 1854. The music continued to gain popularity and in the 20th century was exploited by Trujillo for political purposes. Trujillo appreciated the appeal of merengue for the rural majority and used it to draw large crowds to his political meetings and demonstrations. He ordered merengue to be played on government radio stations along with his version of news and political propaganda, thereby further increasing his control over the country. Trujillo himself was known as an indefatigable merengue dancer.

Visitors to the Dominican Republic will soon realize that merengue is truly a national obsession, whether they first encounter it live at the airport, in their hotels, on car radios, on television, or at a disco. The music is powerful and very stimulating, making most people want to get up and dance. Dominicans dance merengue in close pairs, moving primarily with their hips rather than their feet. Locally made percussion instruments such as the *tambora* and the *guira* are still used, and are often supplemented by more high tech instruments such as synthesizers. The mood tends to be all encompassing and the volume is high. Lyrics cover life's basic problems such as love, politics, destiny and (surprisingly often) illegal immigration to the United States.

Traditionally merengue can be divided in three forms, or stages: the *paseo* which sets the mood and starts to develop the musical theme, the *merengue* when the music comes together and the dancing begins, and the *jaleo*, an improvised crescendo a bit like jamming. Merengue is a complex art form and many individuals such as Johnny Ventura or Luis Guerra (of 440 fame) have distinctly different music with a common root. Merengue is a major Dominican export and is increasingly popular in the United States and Europe. Visitors who enjoy music and dancing should make merengue a central part of their nocturnal activities in Santo Domingo. Merengue predominates at most of the night stops listed below.

Bars and Discos

Santo Domingo
Santo Domingo has an active nightlife with good shows and enjoyable musical revues. Discos often have local and foreign entertainers. Most major hotels have attractive piano bars with happy hours during the week, generally from 6pm–8pm.

Drakes's Pub, La Atarazana, in the colonial zone near the Alcazar, named after Santo Domingo's nemesis, has a 16th century ambiance

Raffles, Av. Hostos, classy bar across from ruins of Hospital San Nicolas de Bari in the colonial zone, Bohemian ambiance, good music (merengue, jazz reggae) and generous drinks, pool tables for players

Village Pub, Av. Hostos 350, 688-7340 (next to Raffles)

Blues Bar, George Washington Av. (on the Malecon), happy hour 5pm–8pm, seafront establishment with outdoor terrace, jazz

D'Golden Club, 14 Roberto Pastoriza Av., 565-2616, exclusive bar with an older, more sophisticated crowd

Cafe Atlantico, Av. Mexico corner Abraham Lincoln, 565-1841, very popular nightspot among young people, live music Monday nights, also a good restaurant, happy hour daily 5:30pm–8:30pm

Grand Cafe, Lope de Vega, live music, relaxing and informal atmosphere

Maunaloa, Centro de los Heroes, 532-3207, live music and shows, formal dress, cover charge

OH-Bar, in the Hotel Dominican Fiesta, 562-8222, Tues.–Sun., 6pm–2am, intimate atmosphere with live music nightly

Las Palmas, located in Hotel Santo Domingo, 535-1511, 6pm–12pm and happy hour, 6pm–8pm, designed by Dominican born Oscar de la Renta, elegant piano bar with small dance floor, live music nightly and entertainment on weekends, no cover charge

El Yarey, Hotel Sheraton, 685-5151, 10am–2am and happy hour daily 6pm–8pm, relaxed atmosphere with view of the ocean, live music and dancing daily, Fri./Sat shows with cover charge

Embassy Club, located in the Hotel Embajador, Sarasota Av., 533–2131, formal setting, jacket required, happy hour Mon.–Fri. 6–8pm, live entertainment

Le Petit Chateau, ocean front location along Autopista 30 de

Mayo, 11.5 km out of town, 535-7262, adult entertainment, center dance stage; show is choreographed and costumed; food and drink are available

Number One, located in Hotel Embajador, adult entertainment, live shows nightly, lounge atmosphere

La Mancha, pleasant bar located in the Hotel Lina, 563-5000

Hispaniola Bar, located in Hotel Hispaniola, Abraham Lincoln and Independencia, 535-7111, Mon.–Wed. 5:30pm–1:30pm, Thurs.–Sat. 5:30pm–2:30pm, happy hour Mon.–Sat. 7pm–9pm; dancing to live music nightly in relaxing atmosphere, no cover charge, free snacks

L'Azotea, located in Hotel Dominican Fiesta, 562-8222, Fri.–Sun.: 8pm–2am, happy hour 8pm–10pm, rooftop nightspot with beautiful view, live music and entertainment, elegant atmosphere, jacket required

Xenox, 13 Ortega y Gasset, 565-8222, bar with shows and live music

Omni, disco located in the Hotel Sheraton, 685-5151, 8pm–3pm, dance floor can be raised and lowered, good sound system and audiovisuals, live music on Monday, cover charge for live entertainment is RD$ 125–150.

Opus, 624 Independencia Av., 686-2444, trendy nightspot with lots of dancing to the latest music

Babilon, 1005 George Washington Av. (on the Malecon), 542-4851, one of the city's largest and most luxurious discos

Guacara Taina, Mirador del Sur Park, 530-2666, Tues.–Fri. 11pm–dawn, Sat/Sun. 9pm–dawn, unique atmosphere in vast underground cave with the capacity for over 1,000 people, two dance floors with three bars on three levels, cover charge of RD$50 keeps out the riffraff

Neon, located in Hotel Hispaniola, 532-1511, 9–5am, trendy disco, popular with the young, merengue

Bella Blu, George Washington Av. 165, popular disco on the Malecon next to Vesuvios, 689-2911

Safari Disco, on Av. George Washington out toward the western edge of town (near Feria Ganadera) 532-4851

Puerto Plata
Vivaldi Studio, Hermanas Mirabel Str., Disco

La Lechuza (The Owl), Puerto Plata Beach Resort, disco

Playa Dorada
The luxury hotels in the Playa Dorada all provide first class entertainment to their guests.

Sosua
Casa del Sol, disco, said to have the best sound system in the Caribbean.

PJ's International, pub, located in the middle of Sosua's popular restaurants, disco dancing nightly.

Santiago
Disco/Nightclub Riverside, Carretera Janico km 2.5, 583-4788, live entertainment, good music

Disco La Antorcha, Av. 27 de Febrero No. 58, 582-5769, good music, audiovisuals

Camino Real Disco, located on the ground floor of the best hotel in town, large disco popular and convenient for guests

Punta Cana
The luxury hotels along Punta Cana on the eastern edge of the island provide high quality live entertainment to their guests as part of the all inclusive package.

Casinos

Santo Domingo
Casino Hotel San Geronimo, 532-9198, Av. Independencia 1067

Casino Hotel Sheraton, 685-4165, Av. G Washington

Gran Hotel & Casino Lina, 563-4166, Av. Maximo Gomez

Jaragua Resort & Casino, 221-2222, Av. G Washington 367,

Naco Hotel & Casino, 562-3100, Av. Tiradentes 22,

Maunaloa Night Club, 533-2151, C. de Los Heroes

Hotel Hispaniola, 535-7111, Av. Independencia

Puerto Plata
Jack Tar Village Resort & Casino, 586-3800

Playa Dorado Hotel & Casino, 562-2774

Puerto Plata Beach Resort & Casino, 586-4243

Eurotel Playa Dorado Hotel Beach Resort & Casino, 586-3663

Southeast
Hotel & Casino Decameron, 526-2307

Bavaro Beach Resort, 686-5797

Santiago
Hotel & Casino Matum (C), 581-3107

Index

TRAVEL THE WORLD WITH HIPPOCRENE BOOKS!

HIPPOCRENE INSIDER'S GUIDES:
The series which takes you beyond the tourist track to give you an insider's view:

NEPAL
PRAKASH A. RAJ
0091 *ISBN 0-87052-026-1 $9.95 paper*

HUNGARY
NICHOLAS T. PARSONS
0921 *ISBN 0-87052-976-5 $16.95 paper*

ROME
FRANCES D'EMILIO
0520 *ISBN 0-87052-027-X $14.95 paper*

MOSCOW, LENINGRAD AND KIEV (Revised)
YURI FEDOSYUK
0024 *ISBN 0-87052-881-5 $11.95 paper*

PARIS
ELAINE KLEIN
0012 *ISBN 0-87052-876-9 $14.95 paper*

POLAND (Third Revised Edition)
ALEXANDER T. JORDAN
0029 *ISBN 0-87052-880-7 $9.95 paper*

TAHITI (Revised)
VICKI POGGIOLI
0084 *ISBN 0-87052-794-0 $9.95 paper*

THE FRENCH ANTILLES (Revised)
ANDY GERALD GRAVETTE
The Caribbean islands of Guadeloupe, Martinique, St. Bartholomew, and St Martin, and continental Guyane (French Guiana)
0085 ISBN 0-87052-105-5 $11.95 paper

By the same author:

THE NETHERLANDS ANTILLES:
A TRAVELER'S GUIDE
The Caribbean islands of Aruba, Bonaire, Curacao, St. Maarten, St. Eustatius and Saba.
0240 ISBN 0-87052-581-6 $9.95 paper

HIPPOCRENE LANGUAGE AND TRAVEL GUIDES:
Because traveling is twice as much fun if you can meet new people as well as new places!

MEXICO
ILA WARNER
An inside look at verbal and non-verbal communication, with suggestions for sightseeing on and off the beaten track.
0503 ISBN 0-87052-622-7 $14.95 paper

HIPPOCRENE COMPANION GUIDES:
Written by American professors for North Americans who wish to enrich their travel experience with an understanding of local history and culture.

SOUTHERN INDIA
JACK ADLER
Covers the peninsular states of Tamil Nadu, Andhra Pradesh, and Karnataka and highlights Goa, a natural gateway to the south.
0632 ISBN 0-87052-030-X $14.95 paper

AUSTRALIA
GRAEME and TAMSIN NEWMAN
0671 ISBN 0-87052-034-2 $16.95 paper

ELAND
ENRY WEISSER
948 *ISBN 0-87052-633-2* *$14.95 paper*

OLAND
LL STEPHENSON and ALFRED BLOCH
An appealing amalgam of practical information, historical curiosities, and
mantic forays into Polish culture"--*Library Journal*
894 *ISBN 0-87052-636-7* *$11.95 paper*

ORTUGAL
J. KUBIAK
805 *ISBN 0-87052-739-8* *$14.95 paper*

OMANIA
YDLE BRINKLE
851 *ISBN 0-87052-634-0* *$14.95 paper*

HE SOVIET UNION
YDLE BRINKLE
857 *ISBN 0-87052-635-9* *$14.95 paper*

HE CEMETERY BOOK
OM WEIL
he ultimate guide to spirited travel describes burial grounds, catacombs, and
milar travel haunts the world over (or under).
706 *ISBN 0-87052-916-1* *$22.50 cloth*

UIDE TO EAST AFRICA:
NYA, TANZANIA, AND THE SEYCHELLES (Revised)
NA CASIMATI
043 *ISBN 0-87052-883-1* *$14.95 paper*

RAVEL SAFETY:
CURITY AND SAFEGUARDS AT HOME AND ABROAD
ACK ADLER and THOMAS C. TOMPKINS
034 *ISBN 0-87052-884-X* *$8.95 paper*

And three books by GEORGE BLAGOWIDOW to keep you on your toes:

TRAVELER'S TRIVIA TEST:
1,101 QUESTIONS AND ANSWERS FOR THE SOPHSTICATED GLOBETROTTER
0087 ISBN 0-87052-915-3 $6.95 paper

TRAVELER'S I.Q. TEST:
RATE YOUR GLOBETROTTING KNOWLEDGE
0103 ISBN 0-87052-307-4 $6.95 paper

TRAVELER'S CHALLENGE:
SOPHISTICATED GLOBETROTTER'S RECORD BOOK
0398 ISBN 0-87052-248-5 $6.95 paper

TO PURCHASE HIPPOCRENE'S BOOKS contact your local bookstore, or write Hippocrene Books, 171 Madison Avenue, New York, NY 10016. Please enclose check or money order, adding $3 shipping (UPS) for the first book, and 50 cents each of the others.
Write also for our full catalog of maps and foreign language dictionaries and phrasebooks.